Meredith hesita... to interrupt you, but—"

That was as far as she got. Her new client rose from his chair and crossed the room swiftly. Calling her "darling," he pulled her against him and cut off her explanation with a kiss.

She stiffened, but Jeremy Winchester's arms were like steel bands. She was powerless as he molded her body to his hard angles. His mouth possessed hers while his hands moved seductively over her back. A melting awareness spread through her, and she heard bells. A fragment of common sense told her they came from slot machines in the casino, but it didn't seem to matter.

When she stopped resisting, his embrace loosened. Keeping his arm around her, he turned to the men at the table. "Gentlemen, I'd like you to meet my fiancée."

Meredith could only stare at him in amazement.

Dear Reader,

With her latest novel (of more than fifty!) on the stands this month, award-winning **Nora Roberts** shares her thoughts about Silhouette **Special Edition**:

"I still remember very clearly the feeling I experienced when I sold my first Silhouette **Special Edition**: absolute delight! The **Special Edition** line gave many writers like me an opportunity to grow with the romance genre. These books are indeed special because they allow us to create characters much like ourselves, people we can understand and root for. They are stories of love and hope and commitment. To me, that *is* romance."

Characters you can understand and root for, women and men who share your values, dream your dreams and tap deep inner sources of love and hope—they're a Silhouette **Special Edition** mainstay for six soul-satisfying romances each month. But do other elements—glamorous, faraway settings, intricate, flamboyant plots—sway your reading selections? This month's Silhouette **Special Edition** authors—Nora Roberts, Tracy Sinclair, Kate Meriwether, Pat Warren, Pamela Toth and Laurey Bright—will take you from Arizona to Australia and to points in between, sharing adventures (and misadventures!) of the heart along the way. We hope you'll savor all six novels.

Be like Nora Roberts—share your thoughts about Silhouette **Special Edition**. We welcome your comments.

Warmest wishes,

Leslie Kazanjian, Senior Editor
Silhouette Books
300 East 42nd Street
New York, N.Y. 10017

TRACY SINCLAIR
Sky High

Silhouette Special Edition

Published by Silhouette Books New York

America's Publisher of Contemporary Romance

SILHOUETTE BOOKS
300 East 42nd St., New York, N.Y. 10017

ISBN: 0-373-09512-0

First Silhouette Books printing March 1989

Printed in the U.S.A.

Author of more than twenty Silhouette novels, *TRACY SINCLAIR* also contributes to various magazines and newspapers. She says her years as a photojournalist provided the most exciting adventures—and misadventures—of her life. An extensive traveler—from Alaska to South America, and most places in between—and a dedicated volunteer worker—from suicide-prevention programs to English-as-a-second-language lessons—the California resident has accumulated countless fascinating experiences, settings and acquaintances to draw on in plotting her romances.

Chapter One

I could have gone to Paula's bridal shower for all the good I'm doing around here." Meredith Collins slouched in a chair with her long legs crossed at the ankles, staring moodily out the window.

An older woman continued to work on the ledgers that covered her battered desk. "You can still make it. Why don't you go?"

"We're supposed to be running a business here—although you'd never know it." Meredith stood up and strolled over to the window to watch the small planes taking off and landing on the field outside. "We don't have one charter scheduled for today."

Clara O'Malley glanced up then and gazed at the younger woman fondly. Meredith had been especially blessed by nature—with everything except patience. In jeans and a plaid shirt, she looked much younger than twenty-seven. Some of the customers who chartered their planes for a sight-seeing trip were disconcerted when they discovered Meredith was the pilot. Her professional-looking jumpsuit didn't offset a curling mass of chestnut curls and wide green eyes framed with thick lashes. It drove Meredith wild to be judged by her physical attributes rather than her considerable skill in the air.

"It won't help matters for you to sit around here moping. Go home and change clothes," Clara advised. "If a miracle happens and we get a customer, I can reach you on the beeper."

"That wouldn't be fair. You're the one who ought to take the day off. You have a sick husband. Milt has only been home from the hospital a week."

Clara rolled her eyes. "Is it only a week? God must be punishing me for some terrible sin. I don't know what I'd do if I didn't have an excuse to get out of the house."

Meredith smiled sympathetically. She'd known Milton O'Malley since she was a little girl. He and her late father had been flying buddies and best friends, in spite of the difference in their temperaments. Milt was as explosive as Austin Collins had been calm.

"Is he giving you a bad time?" she asked Clara.

"No worse than an abscessed tooth."

"It must be hard for an active man to be laid up." Meredith's smile faded. "I guess it wouldn't help to tell him that lately we haven't needed his help around here."

"Business will pick up. Before you know it, summer will be here."

"If we could afford a helicopter, we wouldn't have to depend on tourists." Meredith paced the floor distractedly. "We could develop a steady business running a taxi service to the airport and back. Not to mention the income from overnight mail and package delivery. Why are bankers so uncooperative?"

"How do I know? Maybe they're getting even because they weren't allowed to suck their thumbs as children." Clara laughed suddenly. "What we need to look for is a banker with crooked teeth."

"That's not exactly the solution I was hoping for," Meredith remarked dryly.

"It's the best one I can come up with at the moment. Go to your party and let me get this book work done."

Meredith seemed undecided. "Are you sure? I feel guilty about going off and enjoying myself while you're working."

"I'll be able to after you leave," Clara said pointedly.

Meredith looked forward to the shower with mixed emotions as she changed into an amber silk dress that picked up highlights in her chestnut hair. She would be the only "uncommitted" woman at the luncheon. All the others were either married or had formed serious relationships.

Her discontent was irrational, she realized. It wasn't as though she wanted to be married, or that she hadn't had opportunities. What bothered her was the fact that she'd never met that special man who made bells ring. Did such a person exist? Or was she being hopelessly romantic? Meredith sighed as she swept her long hair aside to fasten on gold earrings.

The luncheon was being held in a private room of a restaurant in San Francisco. By the time she'd changed and driven across the Golden Gate Bridge, everyone was having Bloody Marys.

"I'm so happy you made it." Paula rushed over to greet her.

Meredith smiled. "Fortunately, business is bad right now."

"I can't help being glad. Today wouldn't have been the same without my best friend."

They'd grown up together and been roommates in college. "I'm going to miss you," Meredith said fondly.

"Not if you remember to pay your telephone bill. I'll still be at the same number. Just don't hang up if a man answers."

They were joined by Evelyn, another old friend who had married a year earlier. "I suppose the next bridal shower will be given for you," she remarked to Meredith.

"Not unless you can also provide the groom," Meredith answered.

"You've never had any trouble getting dates."

"It's quality that counts, not quantity."

"If you're looking for a man without faults, he doesn't exist," Evelyn advised.

"I beg to differ with you." Paula pretended indignation.

Meredith laughed. "We all know Dennis is perfect, but that doesn't do me any good. He's already taken."

"He has some friends in the district attorney's office who are single. We'll find someone for you," Paula promised.

"I'm not really looking," Meredith protested.

"It never hurts to meet new people." Paula had a speculative look in her eyes, as though she was already going over the list of candidates.

"Lord deliver me from matchmaking friends!" Meredith exclaimed.

"You're safe with me," Evelyn assured her. "All the couples I brought together hated each other on sight. I've decided the whole thing is up to fate, anyway. You meet that special guy when you least expect it. That's the way it was with Don and me. He backed into my car in a parking lot.''

Meredith raised an eyebrow. "Backing into a plane would be a lot more explosive.''

"Don't be so literal,'' Evelyn answered impatiently. "You know what I mean.''

The subject was dropped when they sat down to lunch, much to Meredith's relief. Her friends meant well, but she didn't have faith in either Paula's bachelors or Evelyn's theory of divine intervention. If fate had a Prince Charming earmarked for her, it was taking a long time producing him.

Lunch was over and the bride-to-be was opening her gifts, when Meredith's beeper sounded. She left the room and went to find a telephone.

"How soon can you get back here?'' Clara asked. "We have a customer who wants to fly to Lake Tahoe.''

"Don't let him get away! I'll be there in twenty minutes.'' A glance at her watch told Meredith it was almost two-thirty. "File a three o'clock flight plan, and have Spike gas up the plane.''

"I'd better make it three-thirty to be on the safe side.''

An impatient male voice in the background said, "Is that the best you can do?''

Clara's voice was muffled as she turned her head to answer him. "It is at the last minute like this. All of our pilots are engaged for the day,'' she explained blandly, as though they had a fleet of them. "You're in luck, though. One of our partners is coming in to accommodate you.''

"Tell him I'll want him to wait and bring me back,'' the man said.

Clara hesitated before starting to relay his instructions.

"I heard.'' Meredith stopped her. "How long will he be up there?''

"Wouldn't you say the more the merrier?" Clara asked cryptically.

Meredith knew she was pointing out that the longer he stayed, the more money they'd make. Meredith would have been equally elated if it hadn't been so late in the afternoon. Darkness fell early in winter, and the weather had been bad in the mountains. She didn't relish a night flight in bad weather. Still, they certainly couldn't afford to turn down the business.

"I'll have all that information by the time you get here," Clara said.

Traffic was getting more and more abominable every day, Meredith reflected grimly. It took her almost half an hour to get to the suburban airstrip north of San Francisco where O.M.C. Charter Service was located.

Squealing brakes announced her arrival at the office. She jumped out almost before the motor died, and raced inside with an apology ready.

A tall, dark-haired man turned toward the open door. His expectant expression dimmed when he saw Meredith. "I thought you said twenty minutes." He frowned at Clara. "How much longer is the pilot going to be?"

Meredith wasn't used to being dismissed that indifferently by a man, but this was clearly no ordinary man. A line from Shakespeare popped into her mind: "Yond Cassius has a lean and hungry look."

Not that she suspected the man of being an assassin. Still there was something about the leashed power in his lithe body, coupled with the intense expression on his rugged face. Those unusual tawny eyes could have belonged to a stalking panther.

"Here's Miss Collins now," Clara said smoothly. "Let me introduce you. Meredith, this is Jeremy Winchester."

He glanced from one to the other with angry incredulity. "You have to be kidding!"

Meredith's placating smile was replaced by annoyance. This one might be extraordinary looking, but he wasn't any different from all the others. "I can assure you I'm a very competent pilot," she stated crisply.

His gaze traveled over her slim body and down the length of her shapely legs, but not with admiration. Meredith relented slightly when she realized a silk dress and spike heels didn't add to her credibility.

"I hope you'll excuse my appearance. I was...I had to attend a business function," she explained lamely. "I'll change and be with you in five minutes."

"How long have you been flying?" he demanded.

She tilted her chin to look squarely at him. "Ten years."

"What did they do, prop you up on pillows?"

"I was seventeen when I soloed the first time." She enjoyed the look of surprise on his face as he did the mental arithmetic. "My father was a pilot. He trained me thoroughly. I've qualified on everything but the large jets."

Jeremy was experiencing frustration—something very foreign to his nature, she surmised. His scowl included both women. "You might have told me what to expect," he growled.

Meredith shared his irritation. How had she considered him attractive? Jeremy Winchester was your standard male chauvinist. "It's your decision," she said coolly. "Do we fly or not?"

"I don't have any choice," he muttered.

She smiled mockingly. "If it will make you feel any better, I'll throw in a parachute—no extra charge."

The flight out, at least, was smooth. Clear skies gave no evidence of the storm that had been predicted. After they were at cruising altitude, Meredith looked back at her passenger.

In spite of the ruckus he'd kicked up, Jeremy wasn't a white-knuckle flyer. The tension evident in him was more likely caused by the papers he had taken out of his brief-case to study broodingly. He didn't even glance out the window.

What was so urgent about this trip to Tahoe? she won-dered. It was merely a resort area near Reno. The only unusual thing about it was its geography. The northern end of the lake was in California, while the southern end was in Nevada. Most of the activity centered around the gambling casinos on the Nevada side.

She'd be surprised if his objective was to visit one of those. He didn't fit the popular conception of a gambler. His dark suit was expensive, yet not flashy, and the only jewelry he wore was a thin gold watch. Maybe he was the head of a syndicate, or an FBI man on the trail of a dan-gerous killer. That covered both extremes.

Meredith knew she was indulging her imagination. He was probably something prosaic like a real estate man trying to close a sale on a piece of property. Her specula-tion was put aside as she monitored landing instructions from the tower at the airfield.

After they landed, Jeremy strode rapidly toward a taxi stand. "Wait for me here," he said over his shoulder.

Meredith ran to catch up. "How long will you be?"

"I don't know."

She looked up at the darkening sky. "Couldn't you give me some idea?"

"I paid in advance," he answered impatiently. "I'm not going to disappear."

"I didn't think you were. I'd just like to know if I should hang around the airport or go into town."

"You're to wait here," he ordered. Before she could reply, he opened the cab door. "The Jackpot Club," he told the driver.

Meredith stared indignantly after the departing taxi. Who did he think she was, his servant? She wasn't used to being ordered around by any man! If it wasn't unprofessional, and they didn't need the money, she'd like to leave him here to find his own way home. Let's see how far he'd get talking to a male airline pilot that way!

She kicked a few stones to let off steam, then went into the terminal. The things to do there were limited. She wandered around the small gift shop for a while, looking at the tacky souvenirs and flipping through magazines and paperback books.

After selecting a romance, she took it into the lounge set aside for pilots. It was empty at the moment. Meredith sighed, poured herself a cup of coffee from a large urn and curled up on a couch with her book.

Time passed slowly. People drifting in and out made it difficult to concentrate on reading, although her preoccupation with the weather prevented that anyway.

"How does it look outside?" she asked a pilot who'd just come in from a flight.

"Lousy, unless you're a skier. There's a front heading this way."

"Snow, or just rain?"

"Snow—lots of it. I'm glad I'm coming in, not going out."

"I'm flying back to San Francisco tonight," Meredith said slowly.

"You'd better hop to it then. If the storm is as bad as they're forecasting, the airport will shut down."

She went to one of the phones and called the airport weather service. The information they gave her confirmed the pilot's warning.

"How long can I count on?" she asked.

"No more than an hour for a small plane," the man replied.

She hung up, biting her lip indecisively. Jeremy had been gone quite a while. He might be on his way back. If she went looking for him they could cross in transit, wasting precious time. But what if he wasn't on his way back? She had to take a chance on going after him, or they'd be stuck here, at least overnight.

The taxi let her off in front of the Jackpot Club, a garishly lit casino. The inside was a kaleidoscope of bright colors: green felt-topped dice and roulette tables, red and blue flashing symbols on slot machines, white balls with black numbers tumbling around in a lotto cage.

Faint strains of music from the cocktail lounge beyond were almost drowned out by the din of excited patrons, and the loud voices of croupiers calling out winning numbers. The rattle of coins clattering into metal cups added to the noise level.

Meredith glanced around with dismay. How would she ever find her passenger in this crowd? On a hunch, she asked a blackjack dealer where the office was. Jeremy might have business there. He would scarcely bring a briefcase if he came to gamble.

The man in the office looked at her without expression. "Jeremy Winchester? Never heard of him."

"I know he came here. A tall man wearing a dark suit with a shirt and tie," she prodded hopefully. The other patrons were dressed much more casually. Jeremy was bound to have been noticed by his clothes alone.

"Lady, do you know how many gamblers we get in here every day?"

"I don't think he came to gamble."

The man's face became even more expressionless, if possible. "What did he come for?"

"I thought he might have an appointment with someone. He was carrying a briefcase."

The man shrugged. "We get all kinds. Sorry, I can't help you."

"Is there anyone else I could talk to? It's really terribly important that I find him. I flew him up here. I'm a charter pilot." To prove she was telling the truth, Meredith rummaged in her purse and brought out her identification. "A storm front is coming in, and the airport's going to shut down. If we don't leave right away, we'll be stranded here."

He examined her pilot's license with narrowed eyes, then dialed a number and listened silently. After replacing the receiver he said, "Okay, that checks out. How much do you know about Winchester's business here?"

So he *did* know him! Why all the secrecy? "Nothing," Meredith answered his question hastily. "I never met him before today. He just walked in and chartered one of our planes. I don't know why he wanted to come here."

"How did you know where to find him?"

"I heard him tell the cabdriver. Look, time is running out," she pleaded desperately. "If you won't let me see him, tell him yourself. We have to be back at the airport in half an hour. I'll wait ten minutes, and then I'm leaving."

The man seemed to be making up his mind. After a nerve-wrenching moment he said, "Okay. Go down the corridor and turn to your left, all the way to the end. Tell the guy at the door to send Winchester out."

Meredith followed his directions, running. When she reached the designated door, she knocked briefly and then opened it. There wasn't time to go through a full-scale interrogation again.

Four men were sitting around a table, while a large burly man stood by the door. Their reactions to her intrusion ran the whole gamut of emotions. Jeremy and the sentry at the door looked apprehensive, and the other three men showed surprise tempered by anger and wariness. A daunting aura of menace clung to all of them.

Meredith hesitated. "I'm sorry to interrupt you, but—"

That was as far as she got. Jeremy had risen from his chair and crossed the room swiftly. Before she knew what he intended, he called her "darling," pulled her against him and cut off her explanation with a kiss.

She stiffened indignantly, but his arms were like steel bands. She was powerless as he molded her body to his hard angles. For what seemed an eternity but was probably only a few seconds, his mouth possessed hers while his hands moved seductively over her back. A melting awareness spread through her body, and she heard bells. A fragment of common sense told her they came from slot machines in the casino, but it didn't seem to matter.

When she stopped resisting, Jeremy's embrace loosened. His mouth trailed up to her ear, but his murmured words jolted her back to reality.

"Do exactly as I say, or you'll regret it." His voice was a faint whisper.

As she stared at him in shock, one of the men at the table said, "What the hell is going on? This meeting was supposed to be private. What's she doing here?" His voice was hard.

Jeremy turned to face the others, keeping his arm around her. "Gentlemen, I'd like you to meet my fiancée." When Meredith stared at him in amazement, his eyes blazed for an instant in warning.

"Congratulations," said the man who seemed to speak for all of them. He was in his middle forties, with a face that appeared to be carved out of granite. "I repeat, what's she doing here?"

Jeremy chuckled. "I guess I left her alone too long. Didn't I, baby?"

"No, I...uh...yes," she finished lamely, sensing she'd better follow his lead.

"Who do you think you're conning? I don't buy this for a minute," the spokesman at the table stated.

"That's because you've never been in love, Al," Jeremy answered. To Meredith he said, "Wait outside for me, sweetheart. I'll be along as soon as I can."

The man at the door took a step forward, looking at Al, who shook his head imperceptibly. Meredith's feeling of unreality deepened as she realized they weren't going to let her leave.

"What are you trying to pull, Jerry?" Al asked.

"Nothing! Why so jittery?"

"I don't like surprises, and I don't think she barged in here because she suddenly got the hots for you," Al answered cynically. "You'd better come up with a story I'll believe, or I'm going to be very displeased with you."

Meredith knew it was time to back up Jeremy's story. She gazed at the men with wide innocent eyes. "I hope I haven't gotten Jerry into any trouble. He told me to wait for him, but I had to tell him about the snowstorm." She turned the same limpid gaze on Jeremy. "If we don't leave right away, sugar, we're going to be stuck here for days."

He relaxed a fraction. "My little doll is a pilot," he told the men proudly. "She flew me up here in her own plane."

Meredith could tell from the way they inspected her that her jumpsuit with the firm's logo gave credence to his story. She pressed the advantage. "I don't mean to rush you, but I have to get back. If you'd like to stay on, maybe I could pick you up when the weather clears."

"That might be best," Jeremy agreed casually.

After a moment's silence Al said, "No, you'd better go with her. We're just about finished here, and you do have that little matter to take care of."

Meredith didn't wait for him to change his mind. "I'll go out and flag down a cab," she said.

Reaction had set in by the time Jeremy appeared, leaving her furious. He was barely settled inside the taxi when she lit into him.

"What did you get me into? I run a respectable charter service. If I'd known you were a gangster, I'd never have agreed to bring you here!" she raged.

He seemed to have trouble restraining himself. "I *paid* for the privilege. I also left instructions, which you didn't follow."

"You have no right to tell me what to do."

He swore under his breath. "I knew you were trouble the minute I laid eyes on you."

She gasped with indignation. "*You're* the one who got *me* mixed up in something weird!"

"If you'd done as you were told, none of this would have happened."

"Just exactly what did happen?" she demanded. "Who were those men, and why were they so upset when I showed up?"

His expression was formidable. "None of this concerns you."

"That's where you're wrong, buddy," she answered grimly. "I want to know what you're involved in. That wasn't a fraternity beer bust you were attending."

"It was a business meeting—which you'd do well to forget about."

Meredith's chest felt suddenly constricted as a possibility occurred to her. "Were you dealing drugs in there?"

His complete astonishment convinced her more than his denial. "Of course not! Where did you get an idea like that?"

"Maybe when Big Al threatened to leave your footprints in cement, along with the rest of you."

"My God, I've got a teenage cop show freak on my hands!"

"All right, so he didn't say it in so many words, but his meaning was clear. He wasn't promising to take you to the movies," she said darkly.

Jeremy gritted his teeth in an attempt to contain his irritation and speak reasonably. "Al is a very...impatient man. The only thing he was threatening to do was back out of our deal."

"What kind of deal? Why would he call it off just because I found out?"

"You haven't found out anything, so don't pretend you have," Jeremy warned. "You could be very, very sorry."

He'd said as much after he'd kissed her. She had intended to read the riot act to him about that, too, but as she gazed at the powerfully built man beside her, a cold chill ran up her spine. A million questions remained, yet Meredith wasn't sure she wanted the answers. Jeremy might not be a drug dealer, but that left numerous unsavory occupations. The most unpalatable one that came to mind was paid assassin. Could her first impression of him have been correct?

They drove the last mile to the airport in silence. Meredith sat huddled in a corner of the seat, as far from her brooding companion as possible, although he seemed to have forgotten her existence.

When they reached the airfield he reached for her arm to help her out. It was merely an absentminded courtesy, but she flinched away. A strange emotion darkened his tawny eyes at her reaction. Was it regret? Meredith's mouth became dry. What did he intend to do to her?

Fortunately, filling out the flight papers and checking with the tower and ground crew drove Jeremy out of her mind for the moment. The weather was worsening, and she would need her wits about her.

One of the mechanics advised her not to leave. "You'll be caught in the middle of the storm."

"Only for a short time."

"Did you get a reading on those winds?" he asked.

"I have clearance. They wouldn't give it to me if it wasn't safe."

Jeremy joined her on the tarmac. "Any problem?"

"It's apt to be a rough trip," she said. "Maybe you'd better stay over, after all." The chance to get rid of him seemed heaven-sent.

"Are you going?"

"Yes, I . . . I have to get the plane back. We have some charters tomorrow morning," she lied.

"Okay, then I'll go with you."

"I honestly wouldn't advise it," she said earnestly. "You'd be much better off taking a scheduled flight. We'll refund your money, of course."

His smile was mirthless, as though he saw through her plan. "I'm not worried about the money."

When a snowflake settled on her eyelashes, Meredith turned away. She didn't have time to argue. "Well, if that's the way you feel, it's your funeral," she muttered.

"I hope not, because then it would be your funeral, too, and that would be a pity."

She jerked her head up to stare at him, but the only emotion she could detect in his golden eyes was something that looked like amusement.

The flight proved to be a nightmare. The full force of the storm hit them within fifteen minutes of leaving the ground. At the cruising altitude assigned to her, the little plane was tossed around like a Ping-Pong ball. She could have requested permission to climb higher, but it wouldn't have done any good. The light aircraft didn't have the capability to rise above the turbulence.

Meredith gritted her teeth and prepared to ride out the storm. She'd flown in bad weather before, but never anything like this. What she desperately needed was a copilot. Keeping the buffeted plane steady took all her concentration, yet so many other things required monitoring.

She'd forgotten all about Jeremy until he eased himself into the seat next to her and buckled himself in.

"Are we in trouble?" The question was asked calmly, although apprehension would have been completely understandable. The plane had just taken a shuddering drop.

"No, we'll make it." Meredith tried to hang on to the bucking rudder with one hand while she reached with the other to adjust a dial.

"Is there anything I can do to help?" he asked quietly.

"Do you know anything about flying?"

"No, but I can follow instructions—unlike some people."

She spared a moment to look at him with grudging respect. If he could joke at a time like this when most people would be terrified, Jeremy Winchester couldn't be all bad.

"Okay, you just won your copilot wings," she said crisply. "Watch the magnetic stabilizer—that gadget on the right. When the dial drops below the median line, bring it back to center."

"Got it. What else?"

"Give me an altitude reading every thirty seconds so I don't stray off course."

The next half hour was a blur of activity. They functioned together as a well-trained team, making Meredith's job infinitely easier. In the fleeting moments that she had to think about it, she marveled at how competently Jeremy did his part.

As they flew farther west, the fury of the storm abated and they had a chance to relax. The softly lit cockpit took on a cozy atmosphere that created an air of comradeship.

"Well, we made it, partner." Meredith flexed her tired shoulder muscles.

"Didn't you expect to?"

"Certainly I did. I wouldn't have gone up otherwise. A responsible pilot doesn't take chances."

"I thought it might have been worth it to get away from me," he said quietly.

Was clairvoyance another of his talents? She tried to turn the suggestion into a joke. "Why would I want to do that? I'd have to refund your money."

His face remained serious. "I can't supply the answers you're looking for, Meredith, but I'd like you to know you have nothing to fear from me."

There was no reason to believe him, but she did. "I know that," she murmured.

"I'd give anything if this hadn't happened."

"Did I really spoil things for you?"

"That wasn't what—" He stopped abruptly.

"You don't think those men believed I was your fiancée," she said slowly.

A smile lightened his soberness. "You were very cooperative. I want to thank you."

She directed her eyes toward the instrument panel so she wouldn't have to look at him. That stirring moment in his arms had acquainted her with every hard muscle in the long body sprawled out next to her.

"I'm glad my performance was adequate," she said lightly.

"I'm only sorry I couldn't give it the attention it deserved."

If that kiss took only part of his concentration, Meredith's head spun to think what he could do if he really put his mind to it! "It wasn't the best of circumstances," she answered.

"No," he said regretfully. "I wish we could have met at a different time, in a different place."

"Do you have to go through with this, whatever it is?" she asked impulsively. "Can't you get out?"

"No." His generous mouth thinned.

"You're not like those men," she said urgently. "But if you continue to do business with them, you'll wind up as hardened as they are. Is money really worth that?"

"What makes you think I'm motivated by money?"

"What other reason could you have for associating with thugs? And don't tell me I've been watching too much television. Those men are dangerous!"

Jeremy's expression was once more withdrawn. "That's why you're going to forget all about tonight."

"You admit it, then!"

He hesitated. "Sometimes things aren't exactly as they seem."

"You mean the four of you were actually planning a charity benefit—including the guard dog at the door?" she asked derisively.

"Don't open Pandora's box, Meredith." His face was stern.

She felt the need to justify herself. "It's not just curiosity. I have the feeling you're in over your head."

"Why should you care?"

"I wouldn't have earlier," she admitted. "I thought you were the worst kind of male chauvinist. But I saw a different side of you this past hour. You showed intelligence and courage. I hate to see all that potential wasted."

"You're very sweet," he said huskily. "I feel guilty about misjudging you, too."

"In what way?"

"I thought you were one of those women who get by on their beauty alone."

Meredith hid her gratification behind a dry manner. "You didn't seem overly impressed."

He smiled. "Under different circumstances I would have regarded you as a challenge."

That reminded her of his situation. "Can't you see those circumstances are altering your life?"

He studied her classic features, illuminated by the lights of the control panel. Some deep emotion darkened the gold in his hazel eyes. "Don't rush to judgment, Meredith. Most of us lead sheltered lives, even the most sophisticated of us. The weaknesses that decent men fall prey to are incomprehensible to a lot of people who have never been tempted."

Was Jeremy an addict instead of a dealer? Meredith rejected the notion as soon as it surfaced. Those steady hands and clear eyes and that decisive manner didn't belong to an addict. He was hooked in some way, though.

"I suppose you have to do what you think best," she said in a muted voice.

"That's all any of us can do," he answered simply.

The lights of San Francisco appeared on the horizon. For the next fifteen minutes Meredith was busy on the radio. The short period of intimacy was over.

After they landed Jeremy stood next to her, alongside the plane. "It's been a memorable experience," he told her with a smile.

"For me, too. Would you like a cup of coffee to sort of unwind?" she asked, aware that she was trying to detain him.

"Thanks, but I have an appointment."

"Oh...well, sure...it was just a thought."

"A very nice one." He took both her hands and squeezed them. "Happy landings, Meredith."

"You, too," she murmured wistfully, watching him stride away across the tarmac.

The only man who had ever stirred her senses this powerfully disappeared into the fog that hugged the airport. One moment he was a vibrant presence, the next a mere figure out of a romantic dream.

Meredith sighed as she turned toward the office.

Chapter Two

Meredith was surprised to find Clara still at her desk. "What are you doing here at this hour?" she exclaimed.

"I wanted to be sure you got back all right. The weather report wasn't good."

"That's an understatement! I learned the true meaning of rock and roll."

"Why didn't you stay over?"

"Our client had a round-trip ticket," Meredith reminded her.

"Handsome devil, wasn't he? But tense as a tiger. He made Milt look like a pussycat." Clara laughed.

"If you don't go home soon, your pussycat will be clawing the furniture."

"He will be, anyway. Never marry a man who thinks patience is an old-fashioned girl's name."

"Don't be too hard on him. Those broken ribs must be pretty uncomfortable."

"He could stand the pain a lot better if he'd broken them in a more macho way than slipping in the bathtub," Clara remarked dryly.

Meredith grinned. "I'll tell that to all the people who consider flying dangerous."

"Did your passenger turn pale and promise to atone for all his sins when the weather got tough?"

"No, he was quite calm."

"That's good. You can never tell about those strong, silent types. Sometimes they unravel like a cheap sweater."

Meredith couldn't imagine Jeremy in less than full control, but she was curiously reluctant to tell what she knew about him. Instead, she pretended a mild interest.

"Did he tell you anything about himself while he was waiting?" she asked casually.

"Mostly he wore a path in the carpet—when he wasn't looking at his watch. You'd think a jealous husband was on his trail."

"Or the police. But in that case, he wouldn't have returned," Meredith mused incautiously.

The older woman looked startled. "You don't think he was a criminal?"

"No, certainly not."

Meredith tried to put conviction in her voice, although she couldn't imagine why she was shielding him. Clara was her friend and partner. She was entitled to all the facts. But there weren't any, only vague suppositions that might worry her needlessly.

Clara frowned. "His behavior was rather strange, though. Did *you* find out anything about him?"

"Just that he had business in Tahoe."

"What kind?"

"I don't know. What does the consent form say he does for a living?"

Although no charter service liked to bring it to a customer's attention, they had to have pertinent information in case of accident. Instead of coming right out and asking whom to notify, the form contained a lot of extraneous questions: age, occupation, business address and telephone number, etc.

"We'll soon find out." Clara rummaged briefly through the papers on her desk. She held up the applicable one with a triumphant expression that dimmed when she started to read it.

"What did he put down?" Meredith asked.

"Not much. Just his name and address—not even a telephone number."

"How about next of kin? That's the whole purpose of the thing."

Clara shook her head. "Every space is blank except the two things I told you."

"How could you let him get away with that?"

"I was so pressed for time," Clara answered defensively. "The plane had to be serviced, and all the paperwork filled out. I had just finished when you arrived."

Jeremy Winchester was getting more and more mysterious every minute. Meredith had tried to give him the benefit of the doubt, but if he had nothing to hide, why hadn't he filled out the form?

"At least he lives in a nice neighborhood," Clara said. "Two-fourteen Broadtree—that's in Pacific Heights. Perhaps he just felt the questions were irrelevant—which they are. We've had customers who objected before."

"Maybe you're right," Meredith answered without conviction.

"It doesn't matter now, anyway. As long as you're back safe and sound, I'm going to leave before Milt sends out a search party."

"Give him my love," Meredith replied absently.

"You should go home, too. You've had a long day."

Meredith's mouth curved ruefully. "Yes, it's been very eventful."

"Don't worry about Jeremy Winchester," Clara advised. "If he *was* up to something, it will remain his little secret. We'll never see him again."

Meredith stifled a sigh. "I'm sure you're right."

When she first started to suspect someone was following her, Meredith told herself she was imagining things. The plain black sedan she glimpsed in her rearview mirror now and then was so nondescript it could have been any one of several different cars of the same make. No distinguishing marks identified it as the same car every time. Besides, why would anyone want to follow her? It made her uneasy, though. All kinds of nuts roamed the streets these days.

Her increased awareness caused her to notice a black sedan that followed her into the parking lot when she stopped at a market on her way home from work. It parked some distance away, but she could see the driver was a man. Not anyone she recognized, although he was several lanes away.

Before she could try for a better look, he opened a newspaper in front of his face. That didn't prove anything, either. He could be a perfectly innocent husband, waiting to pick up his wife.

The car was still there when Meredith came out with her groceries. When she started her motor, the driver started his, too. That was proof her imagination wasn't working overtime. Who was he, and what did he want? A tiny finger of fear touched her spine.

Then came the phone calls. At first they didn't seem connected in any way. They annoyed rather than disturbed her. One was from a local department store.

"We have your name down in our bridal registry," the saleswoman said. "But I don't see any record of your preference in china and silver. Could you come down at your earliest convenience and select your patterns?"

"I'm afraid you've made a mistake," Meredith told her.

"Isn't this Meredith Collins, 418 Cloverdale Drive?"

"Yes, but I didn't—" Meredith stopped abruptly. Coming so soon after Paula's shower, this sounded like some of her practical-joking friends. "I've changed my mind about registering," she told the woman. "Tell any of my friends who inquire that I'd prefer a large check instead." She hung up, chuckling at the thought of the woman's shocked disapproval.

When she received a phone call from a man who said he was conducting a city survey to select prospective jurors, Meredith had no reason to connect the two calls. She gave her vital statistics—name, age and occupation. Then the questions became more probing.

"Have you ever worked for the police department, Miss Collins, local or federal?"

"No."

"How about the Treasury Department?"

"No, I've always been in aviation, except for some minor jobs in college."

"You've never been connected with any branch of government?"

"I already told you. Why do—"

"Are you making any payments on a house, a car or perhaps personal possessions?" he continued crisply.

"I don't own a house, but I'm paying on my car," she answered slowly.

"How about doctor bills, or other liabilities?"

Meredith frowned. "These are very personal questions. I don't see what they have to do with my ability to serve on a jury. What department did you say you're from?"

"You've been very cooperative, Miss Collins," he answered smoothly. "I'm sorry to have taken up so much of your time. Have a nice day."

Something about his hasty retreat didn't ring true. She had a feeling of sinking in quicksand. Too many strange things were happening. She brooded for a few moments, then dialed Paula's number.

After they'd discussed the shower, Meredith said, "I'd like you to ask Dennis something for me."

"He's right here—you can ask him yourself."

"What can I do for you?" he asked cheerfully when Paula turned the phone over to him. "Do you have someone you want prosecuted?"

"Lots of people—mostly bankers who won't lend money."

Dennis laughed. "We'd never have time for the criminals. What else is bothering you?"

"I got a strange telephone call," she said, her face sobering. "At least I think it was strange. Are these questions usual?" She told him what she'd been asked.

"Absolutely not! Who did this man say he was?"

"He didn't give his name. He just said he was doing a survey on prospective jurors."

"For one thing, it isn't done over the phone. You're mailed a notice to appear at City Hall, or the Hall of Justice. For another thing, you don't have to fill out anything. You aren't even asked any questions until you're impaneled for a jury. And neither the district attorney nor the defense counsel would ever ask things like that.''

''I didn't think so. What do you think it means?''

''I don't know. Maybe it's some shady loan company that's going to try a pitch on you to borrow money if they think you're good for it. Or it could be a fly-by-night stock company. At any rate, if they contact you again, try to get the man's name and a number where you can call him back. This is the sort of thing we try to nip in the bud.''

''You think it's some kind of scam?''

''I'm sure of it. Keep me posted.''

Meredith should have been reassured after she hung up, but she wasn't. Maybe it would have been wise to tell Dennis about the man who was following her. If she was wrong, though, she'd look paranoid.

During a sleepless night Meredith acknowledged that she had a problem, and it wasn't in her mind. She even knew the source. All of the weird things that were plaguing her had happened after she flew Jeremy to Tahoe.

All of this was tied up with him somehow. The phone call from the department store hadn't been a practical joke. He'd told those men she was his fiancée, and they were checking up. But what possible difference could it make whether she was engaged to Jeremy or not?

The questions on the survey about her connection with the government were more understandable. They wanted to know if she was a police informant. Suddenly Meredith got a glimmering. If she was married to Jeremy, she couldn't testify against him.

But why did they want to know her financial position? Were they prepared to offer her a bribe to back off? From what? Meredith wondered in frustration. The one who could tell her was Jeremy. She punched her pillow forcefully. Tomorrow he was going to clear up this mystery or she'd take it to the police. She'd put up with enough because of him!

Meredith had two charters scheduled the next day. The revenue was welcome, yet she found it difficult to concentrate on her usual monologue.

"We're flying over San Francisco Bay, ladies and gentlemen. Below us is Angel Island," she said mechanically. "The area is a wildlife refuge and national park now, but during World War Two it served as an embarkation point for thousands of servicemen on their way to the Pacific."

"Excuse me, but isn't that Alcatraz?" one of the men in the group asked.

Meredith gathered her wandering thoughts. "Oh...uh...yes, you're right. I was referring to the island in the distance. The one directly below us is Alcatraz. You can see the former gun turrets and walkways for the guards. No successful escape was ever documented."

"It's so close to shore," a woman remarked. "You'd think a convict could have swum that distance easily."

"Some tried it, but the water is very cold all year round, and the currents are extremely strong. If a swimmer wasn't numbed by the cold or swept out to sea, he could fall victim to a shark attack. Many varieties of sharks infest the waters, including an occasional great white."

The tourists shuddered in happy fascination as they peered down at the choppy waters surrounding the grim stone prison. Some were convinced they could see the triangular black fin of a killer shark.

Meredith's tour took them over North Beach, where bohemians frequented coffeehouses to read their poetry. The wide streets changed to narrow, crowded ones when they passed over Chinatown. The contrast between Oriental architecture and modern downtown skyscrapers only a few blocks away was especially marked.

She dutifully pointed out Grace Cathedral and the plush hotels atop Nob Hill before turning west to swing over the outlying neighborhoods.

"Those homes down there are gorgeous!" a woman passenger exclaimed, staring at the large houses surrounded by carefully tended lawns and gardens. "What do you call this part of town?"

"Pacific Heights," Meredith answered. "It's one of our finest residential areas."

"I'll bet! Have you ever been inside one of those houses?"

"No, but I will be tonight." Meredith's chin set firmly.

The early darkness of winter had fallen by the time she parked in front of Jeremy's house on a broad, tree-lined street. It was a relief to see lights inside the stately brick Tudor mansion. She'd been prepared to wait outside until he came home, if necessary, but the knowledge that she was being followed again would have made the wait nerve-racking.

She hurried up the walk, feeling vulnerable in the darkness. Was this the chance the man in the black sedan was waiting for? Her heart was pounding as she pressed the doorbell.

Jeremy's greeting was less than cordial. "What are you doing here?" he demanded.

"You do remember me, then?" she asked acidly.

"Of course I remember you, but what are you doing here?" he repeated.

"I've come for some answers—and this time I won't be put off."

"Go away, Meredith. Forget you ever met me!"

"I'll be glad to if you'll tell your friend to call off his goon squad."

"What are you talking about?"

"Don't play innocent with me," she said angrily. "I want to know why I'm being followed."

Jeremy's long body tensed as he looked beyond her to the darkened street.

"The black sedan parked down the block—as if you didn't know," she added cynically.

He took her arm and pulled her inside, closing the door. "Are you sure about this?"

"Of course I'm sure! It's been going on for days, and I want it to stop!"

"Have you told anyone about this?" he asked.

"No, but I will unless you level with me," she warned. "I want to know who you are and what business you're in."

He stared at her with an unreadable expression on his face. The only thing she could tell was that furious thoughts were coursing through his mind. Finally he said, "Come into the living room."

They'd been standing in a gracious entry hall lit by a crystal chandelier. As she followed Jeremy into an opulent living room, Meredith had a swift impression of rich paintings on the walls, and a curving staircase leading to an upper floor.

"Would you care for a drink?" he asked.

"No, this isn't a social call," she replied curtly.

He smiled charmingly. "We could still have a drink."

"It won't do you any good to stall. I'm not leaving here until I get some answers. What's the matter?" she asked sharply as his gaze became fixed.

"You have something caught in your eyelashes." When she brushed at them ineffectually he said, "Don't do that, you'll get it in your eye. Come over here to the light." He led her to a lamp by a front window. "Look up at me."

His back was to the window as he lifted her chin in his palm and bent his head down to hers, close enough so she could feel his warm breath on her skin. Meredith stiffened, thinking he was going to kiss her. But he flicked her eyelashes briefly, then raised his head.

"There, it's gone," he said.

"Thank you. Now can we get back to the subject?"

"Let's discuss it over coffee, since you won't have a drink."

Her green eyes sparkled dangerously. "I'm prepared to stay here all night if that's what it takes."

He moved very close. "I don't consider that a threat."

The house was ominously silent. There didn't seem to be anyone else about, not even servants. Normally, Meredith might have been slightly apprehensive at the situation. Jeremy's lean, taut body was daunting at any time, and even more so when he was being seductive, like now. Yet she had the strangest feeling that it was all an act.

She stood her ground and looked up at him. "It wouldn't be a night to put in your memory book."

Admiration warmed his eyes. "Okay, you win. Indulge me in just one thing. I really do want a cup of coffee. Will you join me?"

She examined the invitation for tricks, without finding any. "I suppose so."

"Good, let's go into the kitchen. Do you know how to make coffee? My housekeeper's on vacation."

Meredith smiled unwillingly. "You're a real manipulator. What would you have done if I wasn't here?"

"Made instant, but I detest the stuff."

She was mildly surprised when he turned off all the lights in the living room before they left. It seemed like a small economy for a man wealthy enough to live in a house like this. But rich people had their quirks like anyone else, she supposed.

He led her to a large modern kitchen at the back of the house. After pointing out the coffee maker he said, "I guess you can figure out what to do with that. If you'll excuse me for a moment, I'll be right back." He disappeared before she could ask where the coffee was kept.

Leaving Meredith to rummage through cupboards, Jeremy went swiftly to the entry hall and turned off the lights, plunging the lower floor into darkness. He ascended the staircase by the light coming from the master bedroom at the front of the house.

Meredith would have had second thoughts if she'd observed his actions. After taking off his jacket in front of the uncurtained window, he reached up to loosen his tie with one hand while he closed the drapes with the other. Unaccountably, he put on his jacket again, went to the door and turned off the bedroom lights, too.

His tall figure merged with the darkness as he moved to the top of the steps, becoming merely a fluid shadow gliding noiselessly down the staircase.

Meredith jumped as Jeremy appeared behind her. "You startled me! Do you always move so quietly?"

"It's a talent that comes in handy for pouncing on beautiful women."

"Compliments won't get you anywhere," she stated flatly.

"I was afraid of that. You're a very determined woman."

"You'd better believe it!" She poured two cups of coffee, carried them to the kitchen table and sat down. "All right—talk."

He took the chair across from her. "What do you want to know?"

"Who are you, for starters. Is Jeremy Winchester your real name?"

"Yes."

"What business are you in?"

"I'm a banker."

Meredith's eyes widened. Of all the answers she might have expected, that wasn't one of them. "I don't believe it!"

"Sorry, but it's true."

"What do you do exactly?"

He smiled. "Some of my employees ask the same question."

"You're the boss?" she asked uncertainly.

"I'm the president. Of Northern Pacific Savings and Loan," he added, anticipating her next question.

It was a small but prestigious bank that was on Meredith's list for a loan application. "If you're really who you say you are, why didn't you fill out our questionnaire?" she asked suspiciously.

"I answered the questions I considered relevant."

"Why give your address but not your phone number?"

"So you could bill me in case there were any added charges." His tawny eyes lit with amusement. "I have many faults, but I've never been a deadbeat."

"Okay, that takes care of the minor matters. Now suppose you tell me what a banker would be doing in a casino."

"Aren't we allowed to gamble like anyone else?"

"If that's what you were doing, but you weren't. Why were you there?"

His smile faded. "It happens to be a confidential matter."

"Not when it involves me. Why am I being followed?"

He hesitated. "I'll try to see that you aren't anymore."

"That isn't good enough! It's more than that." She told him about the phone calls. "Those were tied up with this, too, weren't they?"

"It sounds like it," he said reluctantly.

"Wouldn't you say I'm entitled to an explanation?"

After a moment's indecision he said, "I'll have to ask you to keep what I'm about to say in strictest confidence."

"I'll have to hear what it is first."

"Nothing sinister, I assure you. I'm engaged in a business deal with the men you saw at the casino. It's essential that it be kept secret."

"From whom, the police?" she demanded.

"You have a one-track mind," he remarked dryly. "This concerns a place called the Winner's Circle in Las Vegas, a casino that's been badly mismanaged. The owner wants to sell, and Al—the man you saw the other day—wants to buy. But if the news got out that Al was behind the offer, the owner would jack up the price. That's why I asked you to keep this confidential. And why Al was so disturbed when you burst in."

"Who would I tell? I haven't been to Las Vegas in ages. I never even heard of the Winner's Circle."

"He didn't know any of that, including who you were. You could have been anyone from a spy to a reporter."

"Couldn't you have just told him the truth instead of saying I was your fiancée?"

"He might not have believed me. Al doesn't take chances. He could have subjected you to...some very lengthy questioning. But if you were my fiancée, you wouldn't be any threat. Your interests would be the same as mine. It was just a sudden impulse on my part." His eyes took on a deeper glow. "It also gave me a chance to kiss you."

Meredith didn't buy that segment of his explanation. She'd obviously been more affected by that kiss than he. "I don't understand your part in all this."

"My bank is putting up the money."

"I didn't know respectable banks were involved in gambling," she said slowly.

Jeremy's smile was cynical. "We're in business to make money. The recent stock market crash has caused a lot of people to default on their loans. This is a solid investment, a chance to recoup some of our losses." He watched her obliquely. "You see, it isn't very sinister, after all."

"Then why am I being followed?"

"Al doesn't take anyone's story at face value," Jeremy answered simply.

"But that's terrible! What will happen when he finds out you were lying?"

"If you'll cooperate, he won't find out."

"You can't ask me to do that!"

He watched her like a giant cat. "I don't have the benefit of Al's dossier on you. Are you involved with someone else?"

"No, but that doesn't have anything to do with it."

Jeremy's tense body relaxed. He leaned back in the chair and smiled at her. "I thought we got along rather well together."

"When? For one hour in a storm? The rest of the time you were shouting at me."

"And you were shouting back."

She smiled reluctantly. "Well, naturally. Ours would definitely not be a marriage made in heaven."

"We could try being engaged, and see if we can't smooth each other's edges."

"I'm not accustomed to being told I have rough edges," she stated.

"Certainly not visibly." His gaze roamed appreciatively over her curves.

"Don't start taking your role seriously," she warned, although her pulse quickened. "If I agree to this insane notion, it's only in the interests of self-preservation."

"Anything you say," he acceded promptly.

"Are *you* involved with anybody who might take a dim view of our...uh...association?"

"No one."

"You live in this big house alone?"

He grinned wickedly. "Most of the time."

"You'll have to start practicing celibacy," she said tartly. "Big Al is undoubtedly watching you, too. It wouldn't be very credible to be caught cheating on your fiancée."

"If we were really engaged, I wouldn't want to." His voice was like smooth velvet.

"Just remember this is all an act," she said a little breathlessly.

He brought her hand to his mouth and kissed her palm. "One I'm very grateful for."

Meredith pulled her hand away. She still had the feeling Jeremy was playing a part, but her own reaction was all too real. Her body stirred with remembrance as she gazed at his firm mouth and blatantly male frame. What was she letting herself in for? When their usefulness to each other was over, he would walk away unscathed, but would she?

"Is money really worth all this to you?" she asked uncertainly.

A look of tenderness softened the hawklike planes of his face. "Trust me. It's a lot to ask on such short acquaintance, but please believe that I'll never let any harm come to you."

She read truth in his eyes. "I do believe you, Jeremy," she said slowly. "I know firsthand that you're dependable. Your really good qualities just don't seem to jibe with this willingness to do anything for money."

He took both her hands and held them tightly. "All I can tell you is, this is something I have to do."

She smiled uncertainly. "I never had a very high opinion of bankers. Who'd ever have thought I'd be engaged to one?"

His intensity vanished with her tacit acceptance. "What do you have against bankers? We're a fairly jolly group when we're not foreclosing on widows and orphans."

"Or turning down perfectly legitimate loans for small businesses," she said indignantly.

He chuckled. "We're about as popular as the IRS."

"And with good cause! Bankers suffer from myopia."

"Are you speaking from experience, or is this a general indictment?"

"We've been trying to get a loan to buy a helicopter. It would increase our business at least thirty percent, but can we get a banker to listen? No! They operate on the old theory that if you need money you can't borrow it, but if you have enough to buy what you want, they'll loan it to you."

"That's a common complaint. We prefer to call it *required collateral.*"

"A weaseling-out term for what I just said," she answered disgustedly.

"Do you really own that charter firm?"

"Only a third of it. Clara and Milt O'Malley are my partners. Milt and I do the flying, and Clara takes care of the office."

"Is there enough revenue for all of you?"

"It's fallen off lately, along with the economy. That's why we need the chopper, to supplement our income."

"Do you know how to fly one of those things?"

"I can fly anything with wings . . . or rotors."

"I'm not surprised," he said admiringly. "You did an impressive job in that storm."

"You were a big help," she told him.

He smiled. "We're going to make a great team."

"An unlikely one," she said ruefully. "This must be the fastest engagement on record."

"Sometimes it's good to do things impulsively."

"That's strange talk coming from a banker."

"We're human," he assured her. "We work and play and make love like other men."

Not Jeremy. At least not the part about making love. The small sample she'd received told her he'd honed lovemaking to a fine art. He would be thoroughly knowledgeable about what pleased a woman. Meredith's lashes fell as she imagined what it would be like if he really cared about her.

"You don't believe me?" he asked, misinterpreting her silence.

"I was thinking about something else," she answered hastily.

"I hope in time you'll start to see me as a person, with all the failings and strong points of anyone else," he said gently.

"How long will it take to close your deal?" she asked.

"Perhaps three or four weeks."

"That long!"

He looked at her quizzically. "Does it make a difference?"

"I don't suppose so. We won't be seeing that much of each other."

"We will if we want to appear convincing."

"You mean go out on dates and...and stuff like that?"

"I hadn't dared hope for 'stuff like that,'" he teased.

Her fair skin colored. "I meant spend a lot of time together."

"I'll try to see that it isn't a hardship." His golden gaze wandered over her face, lingering on her soft mouth.

Meredith sat up straighter in her chair. "We'd better understand each other right from the start. Our physical contact will be limited to a firm handshake."

"That will look a little strange."

"To whom? Do you think Big Al's goon will keep a report card on us?"

"I was thinking of our friends—yours and mine."

"You expect us to socialize with each other's friends?"

He grinned. "Even engaged couples come up for air."

"That's not one of your better ideas. Our situation is bad enough now, why make it worse?"

"I'm crushed that you couldn't give a convincing performance of being in love with me. That *is* what you're worried about, isn't it?" Amusement sparkled in his eyes.

She frowned at him. "I was referring to the fact that we'd have to answer all kinds of questions—how we met, when we expect to get married, where we're going on our honeymoon."

"We can decide all those things over dinner tomorrow night."

"You're making this needlessly complicated," she insisted.

"We'll need a cover story anyway, in case we bump into someone we know. Why not dream up the perfect scenario? It will be fun," he coaxed. "We'll be the envy of everyone. How many people meet under such adventurous circumstances, are madly in love in a matter of days, and plan to spend an exciting honeymoon in Pago Pago?"

"That doesn't sound very true to life. We'd better argue every now and then for the sake of credibility."

"As long as we kiss and make up. Just joking," he said with a laugh, as she looked at him sharply.

Meredith realized he'd just talked her into something else she didn't want to do. It was time to assert herself. "I'll pretend in front of other people, but I have to tell Milt and Clara the truth."

Jeremy's laughter vanished instantly. "The only way to keep a secret is not to tell *anyone*."

"But they're like family. I don't want them getting all excited over a wedding that's not going to take place."

He sighed deeply. "Well, there goes my deal down the drain."

"They wouldn't tell anyone," Meredith protested.

"Do you really think they could be convincing if Al's people started asking questions?"

Clara might be able to, but Milt was too direct. Neither of them would approve, anyway. Meredith wasn't too comfortable with the idea herself, but it seemed the least she could do, since she was partly responsible for this mess.

"Won't Al be convinced once we start going out together?" she asked tentatively.

"You've met him. What do you think?"

She had a vivid mental picture of the man—cold, hard and suspicious. He'd keep tabs on them until the deal was consummated.

"All right," she said reluctantly. "I won't tell them."

The flare of triumph in Jeremy's eyes was quickly masked. "You don't know how much this means to me."

She shrugged. "I'd hate to see all your efforts go for nothing."

"So would I." The fleeting look on his face chilled her for some reason.

"I'd better go." Meredith stood up.

"I'll walk you to your car."

The front of the house was in total darkness. Feeling her way in the unfamiliar hallway, she bumped into Jeremy. His arms closed around her to steady her.

"Couldn't you afford to leave one little light on?" she asked breathlessly.

His shoulders felt very solid under her clutching hands, and his subtle male scent filled her nostrils. Jeremy Winchester was easily the most overpowering man she'd ever met.

His husky voice had an intimate sound in the darkness. "I turned off all the lights so our silent witness would think we'd gone to bed."

"You tricked me so I couldn't back out!" she said indignantly.

"Because I gave him the impression we were making love?" He laughed softly. "Sweet little Meredith, you're adorable."

She knew what he was saying. They didn't have to be engaged to do that. "Call me hopelessly old-fashioned, but I'd rather look like your fiancée than a one-night stand," she muttered.

"No man could ever get enough of you in one night," he murmured.

She stepped back abruptly. "Will you please turn on the lights so I can see the way to the front door?"

There was no sign of the black sedan outside when Jeremy walked Meredith to her car.

"I'll see you tomorrow," he said. As she started the motor he leaned down and kissed her.

It was a brief kiss, but warm and sweet. She drove away with butterflies fluttering in her stomach, and an appalled sense that she was reacting like a schoolgirl.

Chapter Three

Meredith found it difficult to sleep that night. Jeremy's kiss lingered on her lips like a promise, and she could almost feel the imprint of his hands on her skin. His attraction was magnetic. The fact that it was merely sexual didn't improve matters.

How was she going to put on a convincing act when they were together without getting caught in her own trap? Not that she expected to fall in love with him, but falling into his bed would be equally destructive. She didn't indulge in meaningless affairs—and that was all it would be. Jeremy considered her merely a means to an end. Expecting a relationship to develop under those conditions was unrealistic. He was undeniably fascinating, but there was something vaguely disturbing about him.

Meredith would have been even more disturbed if she'd heard the telephone call he made after she left.

"So that's the story," Jeremy concluded after several minutes. "I thought you should know about the latest developments."

"I don't like it," the man on the other end said. "She spells trouble."

"Not if we can speed things up."

"That would make Al suspicious."

"I suppose so," Jeremy agreed morosely.

"We can't do anything that would make him back out of the deal. Are you sure this girl will go along with you?"

"I don't anticipate any problems. She bought the story."

"Well, just watch your step. Al is a dangerous man to fool with."

"He's a slimy sea slug! I'm enjoying every minute of this double cross."

"Don't get emotional," the man warned. "Remember, we're not just out to fleece him. When we get what we want, he'll be simply a bad memory."

"That's the best part." Jeremy's face was a cruel mask.

"Just see that the girl doesn't get in the way. I'm kind of worried about her. Do you want me to take care of her?"

"Not at this point. I'll let you know if it's necessary."

Jeremy frowned with dissatisfaction as he got ready for bed. "I wish it didn't have to be this way, but it can't be helped," he muttered.

Meredith had taken a long time over her appearance, and the results justified it. She blessed the impulse that had made her splurge on a new black dress. The plunging neckline gave it sophistication, and the short full skirt showed off her legs.

Jeremy's reaction was more than satisfactory when he arrived a short time later. "I definitely got the best part of this deal," he said, staring with frank male appreciation at her lovely face and enticingly curved body.

"Oh, I don't know," she answered lightly. "You might appeal to a certain segment of the female population."

That was an understatement. He was stunningly handsome in a charcoal-gray suit that was expertly tailored to accommodate his wide shoulders. A snowy-white shirt called attention to his deep tan and the unusual color of his eyes.

They were especially golden as he murmured, "I hope you're part of that segment."

"There must be *some* reason why I let you sell me the equivalent of stock in a nonexistent gold mine."

His smile became a little fixed. "Not having second thoughts, are you?"

"No, it's like reading a book. I can never put it down until I find out the ending."

"We're going to live happily ever after, and I'll be the envy of every healthy male in the country," he answered smoothly, putting his arm around her shoulders and leading her out the door.

She looked up at him with a touch of wistfulness. "Only children believe in fairy tales."

"How can we fail? We get to make up our own story."

They had reached the curb where Jeremy's car was parked. It was a red Corvette.

Meredith smiled. "You're already the envy of half the children in the country."

"Why is that?"

"A group of kids were surveyed on what they wanted most in life. Over half of them answered, a red Corvette."

He chuckled. "Are you intimating I'm immature?"

"I doubt if anyone could accuse you of that, but you certainly aren't what you seem."

Something flickered behind his eyes for a moment. "I suppose this car *is* rather flamboyant for a banker."

"You're entitled. Somebody's always ready to criticize. You can't worry about what other people will think as long as it feels right to you."

"My sentiments exactly," he replied evenly.

Over dinner at an excellent restaurant, they discussed the story they planned to tell.

"First of all, how did we meet?" Meredith asked.

"Why not the way we really did? It's better to stick to the truth as much as possible when you're making up a story. You minimize the chances of getting caught in a lie."

"It sounds as though you've had a lot of experience at this sort of thing," she commented.

He shrugged. "No more than the average person, but I'm a gambler. It stands to reason that the odds against you go down when you're not bluffing."

"Do you really gamble—at the casinos, I mean?"

"I've been known to take a fling now and then."

She shook her head wonderingly. "If only you had crooked teeth, you'd be just what I'm looking for."

His gaze was puzzled. "Did I miss something?"

"Never mind, it's a private joke. We'd better get back to business."

"Okay, we've settled on how we met," he said.

"I disagree. What reason would you give for going to Tahoe?"

"I can't imagine anyone asking, but the answer is simple. I went skiing."

"Then why would you have returned the same day? Especially in a snowstorm?"

He looked at her with respect. "You're not bad in the devious department yourself."

"I'm learning from you," she said dryly. "How's this? We met when I came into your bank for a loan."

"We have a loan officer for that. You wouldn't come to me."

"All right, you saw me waiting for my appointment, and fell madly in love with me on the spot."

"That sounds completely believable." His voice deepened.

"Then I'd better not spoil it by saying you gave me the loan." She grinned.

"Bring in your figures, and I'll see what I can do."

"I was only joking, Jeremy!"

He took her hand across the table. "I'd like to do it for you."

"I've been turned down all over town, so it might have to be a personal favor. I don't want it that way."

"Why not? You're doing something for me."

Did he think she expected a payoff? Meredith withdrew her hand. For a short time they'd achieved a feeling of closeness—at least she had. They'd seemed like two friends plotting a mischievous practical joke. But everything was a business proposition to Jeremy—you scratch my back, and I'll scratch yours.

"We'll talk about it later," she said curtly. "Right now we have other things to discuss, and we're not getting very far."

He looked at her speculatively but didn't pursue the matter. "What's next on the agenda?"

"Our wedding date. Women always ask that. Men take the groom aside and offer condolences," she added tartly, still annoyed with him.

Jeremy laughed. "They don't mean anything by it. It's a male ritual, like football players patting each other on the butt to show approval."

"I guess it loses something in the translation. Anyway, when would you like to get married?"

"Isn't that up to the bride?"

"June is a popular month, but it's so traditional."

His eyes sparkled with amusement. "Don't tell me we're going to make up our own vows and recite them in a redwood grove?"

"Why don't we try something really original and get married in the Corvette?"

"It's only a two-seater. Where would we put the minister?"

"I suppose it would scratch the paint if he stood on the hood," she said reflectively.

"Don't even think about it!"

"Well, we can decide on the place later. We haven't picked the date yet."

"Spring would be nice." His eyes roamed over her delicate face. "You could wear a wreath of wildflowers in your hair."

"Orange blossoms are customary."

"We're both nonconformists, deep down." He continued to stare at her consideringly. "I can see you in a pale yellow gown with a bouquet of daffodils in your arms. You'd look like a ray of sunshine."

Whenever she'd thought about getting married, Meredith had always pictured herself in a conventional white gown with the requisite veil cascading down. But Jeremy's vision was more romantic. She gazed at him pensively, seeing herself drifting down an aisle strewn with violets.

"It was just a thought," he said, shattering the image. "I suppose every bride wants to be married in white."

"The first time, anyway."

"You've been married before?"

"No, it was just a commentary on the matrimonial climate today. How about you? Have you ever been married?"

"No."

"How have you managed to stay single so long?"

"I could ask you the same thing."

"Eligible bachelors are scarcer than available women," she said dryly.

"I don't imagine that's ever been a problem for you."

She shrugged, not pretending false modesty. "One of my friends told me I'm too hard to please."

"What are you looking for in a man, Meredith?"

"Merely perfection." She laughed.

"That's in rather short supply." He smiled. "Could you live with perfection?"

"Why not?"

"It would be boring. Would you want a man who was never late to dinner, always remembered your birthday and let you win every argument? You'd know what he was going to do before he did it—even in bed."

"You're thinking negatively," she protested. "What's wrong with being able to depend on someone?"

"Dependability and predictability are two different things. You can depend on a man without having to know what he's thinking at any given moment. It would take all the excitement out of a relationship."

"I didn't say I wanted to know what he was thinking, just that he should be...someone special," she concluded lamely.

"You don't really know what you're looking for, do you?" he asked gently.

Someone who makes my heart sing and the rest of me tingle, she wanted to answer. But that would have sounded childish.

"You'll know when you meet him, honey. And when you do, it won't matter if he forgets to phone or leaves the cap off the toothpaste or keeps you guessing half the time."

"That would make me a victim!"

"Not if you loved each other. He'd put up with the same things from you."

"At least you're assuming this imperfect man loves me back," she said ironically.

"How could he help himself?" Jeremy asked in a husky voice.

"You're just making a case for undependable men because you're one yourself."

"How can you say that? Didn't I show up on time tonight?"

"Yes, but you forgot my birthday."

"When was it?"

"Last month." She smiled.

"A shocking oversight—even though we hadn't met yet. Tell you what. I'll give you a birthday party tomorrow night."

"With balloons and a cake?"

"You've got it."

"That would be nice."

"How did you spend your birthday?" he asked.

"With Clara and Milt. He's laid up with a couple of broken ribs, and Clara works all day at the charter office, so we sent out for pizza."

Jeremy frowned. "That doesn't sound very festive."

"We had champagne first, and Clara put a candle on a cupcake for me."

"Don't you have any family you could have been with?" he asked gently.

She shook her head. "My parents died some time ago, and I was an only child. The few relatives I have live back east." She noticed the expression on his face. "You needn't feel sorry for me. I could have gone out on a date."

"I'm sure you could."

"I chose to be with the O'Malleys because it meant a lot to them. They never had any children of their own, so I'm sort of like their daughter."

"They certainly picked a winner," Jeremy said fondly.

To hide her pleasure at the small compliment she said, "Do you have family?"

"Quite a lot. One set of parents, and two married sisters with children."

"Do they live here?"

"No, one sister lives in Phoenix, the other in Albuquerque. My parents retired to Arizona to be near their grandchildren. They gave up hope of my producing any." He grinned.

"At least you have sisters to do your duty for you." Meredith smiled ruefully. "Clara and Milt won't even be grandparents, technically, but they keep dropping subtle hints about how nice it is to have children while you're young."

"Yours will be even more spoiled than my nieces and nephews."

"If I ever have any," she answered a trifle somberly.

"You and Mr. Perfect will have the national average," he teased. "Two-point-five model children."

"You said I was a rebel," she reminded him. "Maybe I'll have two and three quarters."

"That's the spirit," he approved.

The evening flew by. Meredith enjoyed Jeremy's company, and his admiration was flattering. Of course it was advantageous for him to be nice to her, but she didn't think his compliments were entirely self-serving. There was a definite sexual attraction between them.

It flared openly when he walked her to her door at the end of the evening. His eyes were luminous in the darkness. As she prepared to say goodnight his arms enveloped her, and his head descended, blotting out the moonlight. She lifted her face, undecided whether she wanted to protest or not. When Jeremy's lips touched hers, the question was answered.

A hot flood of desire swept through her as their bodies met and merged. He held her so closely that she was aware of every hard muscle in his lean frame. Her hands moved restlessly over his broad shoulders as his mouth devoured hers. Any vestige of caution was drowned out by the wild beating of her heart.

Jeremy lifted his head and looked down at her with glittering eyes. "You're a love." His voice was a low murmur in her ear. "That ought to fill a page in his notebook."

"What?" His words were incomprehensible.

"Our friend in the black sedan—he's still with us."

"Oh." Meredith felt as though someone had doused her with cold water. She started to turn her head, but Jeremy cupped her chin and turned her face back to his.

"Don't look. We don't want him to know we're onto him," he warned softly. "I'll see you tomorrow night, sweetheart," he continued in a normal voice that carried in the quiet night.

She stood silently as he kissed her again, this time with restraint, and left.

Meredith was grateful that Jeremy thought her cooperation was part of the game they were playing. Hot embarrassment colored her cheeks a vivid pink as she recalled her instantaneous response.

The sexual attraction she'd thought was mutual appeared to be one-sided, however. This was the second time he'd kissed her passionately, and on neither occasion had his emotions been involved.

She flung off her clothes angrily. From now on he could restrict himself to soulful looks to get his point across to their audience! There was a limit to what he could expect her to put up with.

The next morning in the office Clara said, "Come home with me for dinner tonight if you don't have anything else to do. Milt misses you."

"What does the doctor say?" Meredith asked. "Will he be back to work soon?"

"If there's a God in heaven!" Clara answered fervently.

Meredith laughed. "That's nothing but an act you two put on. You'd be lost without each other."

"I don't want to be without him. I only want his disposition to improve."

"It will when he's back in action again. It can't be much longer."

"Not calculated by light-years." Clara smiled. "You're right, I'm exaggerating. But the invitation for dinner still stands."

"Sorry, I have a date tonight."

"Who is it this time, the boring lawyer or the conceited accountant?"

"Neither."

When she didn't elaborate, Clara said, "Not Nathan the nerd? You said you weren't going out with him again."

"I say that about all of them periodically."

"Which one got a second chance?"

"It's . . . uh . . . someone new."

Clara's casual interest quickened. Meredith was usually very open about discussing her boyfriends. Her reluctance this time seemed to indicate this one was special.

"Where did you meet him?" she asked.

Although she'd promised Jeremy—and she realized the wisdom behind his request—Meredith was reluctant to lie to Clara. "I met him in a bank," she mumbled.

"You let someone pick you up?" Clara asked in surprise.

Meredith suppressed a sigh. "He works there."

"You're kidding! I thought you considered bankers one step lower on the evolutionary scale than amoebas."

"Well, he . . . he's different."

"Don't tell me he has crooked teeth?"

Meredith smiled. "Not *that* different."

"I see. You didn't get the loan, but you got the banker as a consolation prize."

"Something like that," Meredith murmured noncommittally.

"In my day banks only gave away calendars," Clara remarked.

"They've gotten more competitive." Meredith stood up. "I'd better get ready for my tourists."

"They won't be here for another hour. Sit down and tell me about this new man." Clara looked at her expectantly.

If she knew the deception would be over soon, Meredith could have invented someone. But the chance that Al's henchmen might find a way to question Clara made that dangerous. She sat down with resignation.

"What's his name, and what does he look like?" Clara asked.

"It's Jeremy Winchester, and you've met him."

"That name does sound familiar." Clara's face cleared as recollection set in, but it was followed by a frown. "Not that autocratic man you flew to Tahoe?"

"That's the one, but he's really quite nice."

"I don't understand." The older woman looked puzzled. "You said he was a banker."

"He is. I just happened to meet him again when I went into his bank for a loan. It was the most amazing coincidence." Meredith hoped her wide-eyed ingenuousness would fool Clara.

It didn't. "*Quite* a coincidence," Clara remarked dryly. "You might almost say it's unbelievable."

"Truth is often stranger than fiction," Meredith answered lamely.

"It certainly is if you're going out with that man. What does he have on you?"

Meredith gave her a startled look. "I don't know what you mean."

"Just a few days ago you were wondering if he was a criminal."

"*You* were the one who thought that."

"And you agreed with me."

"I was tired. I'd just come in from a bad flight. Anything would have spooked me. Jeremy is really quite charming. I . . . uh . . . this is our second date."

Meredith might not have mentioned it at this point, but she had to set the stage for a whirlwind courtship. Clara was already presenting a problem.

The older woman's gaze was troubled. "I know I don't have any right to butt in, but are you sure you know what you're doing? There's something about that man that bothers me."

"It isn't fair to judge somebody by one meeting. He was stressed out, too." Meredith hoped it wouldn't occur to Clara that Jeremy couldn't have known ahead of time the flight was going to be bad.

"I suppose you're right. He must have something if you're dating him two nights in a row. Your standards are pretty high."

"Jeremy lives up to all of them. He's bright, witty, attentive."

"If he's also clean, honest and thrifty, he can get into the Boy Scouts," Clara observed ironically.

"Go ahead and make jokes, but I've never met a man like him before," Meredith said truthfully.

"You're sure your head isn't being turned by just a pretty face?"

Meredith smiled. "You noticed?"

"He's quite a hunk," Clara admitted.

"Yes, he is," Meredith agreed softly.

"Well, watch your step. This Winchester is a different breed of cat than your other boyfriends. You won't be able to lead him around on a leash."

"That will be refreshing," Meredith answered lightly.

Clara looked at her soberly. "I just hope you don't get a dose of your own medicine."

* * *

On their way to the restaurant that evening, Meredith gave Jeremy an edited version of her conversation with Clara.

"You didn't create a great first impression. We'll have to make sure she doesn't see you again."

"On the contrary. I'll have to change her opinion," he answered smoothly.

"Turning on the charm won't get you anywhere with Clara. She's afraid you're going to seduce and abandon me." Meredith laughed.

"Didn't you tell her my intentions were honorable?"

"It was too soon. People don't fall in love that fast."

He turned his head to look at her. "How about love at first sight?"

"That only takes place in romantic novels."

"I imagine it can really happen. But people don't trust their own instincts. They attribute that instant awareness to things like physical attraction or intellectual stimulation."

"It probably is. You can't love someone until you know whether you share the same values and viewpoints."

"That's how you choose a political candidate. You fall in love because you can't help yourself."

The notion was vaguely disturbing to Meredith. "I don't think Clara would buy your concept. She's having enough trouble believing I ran across you again accidentally."

"When she sees how smitten I am, she'll forget all about it."

Meredith frowned. "I hope you don't expect to put on one of your R-rated performances."

"Would I do that in front of your dear old friends?"

"I never know *what* you're going to do," she muttered. "But it has to stop. No more passionate kisses."

"You're taking all the fun out of this," he teased.

"None of it's fun for me," she stated grimly.

Jeremy's face sobered instantly. "I'm sorry. I realize how much you're doing for me."

"I don't really mind," she mumbled. "I just feel uncomfortable about the...the romantic part. We aren't even friends."

"I'd like to think we are. But I want to make this as easy for you as possible." He pulled up to the curb, where a parking attendant was waiting. "I've been guilty of disregarding your feelings, which was thoughtless of me. In the future I promise not to do anything you find distasteful."

His tone was completely serious, but Meredith suspected an underlying mockery. Well, at least she had put an end to his unacceptable behavior.

The restaurant was located on the mezzanine of a new, very exclusive hotel, known for its high prices. The large dining room was filled that evening with elegantly dressed people conversing in carefully modulated voices. Although the food was excellent, Meredith had never cared much for the Delfino Room. The atmosphere was a little too rarefied, as though the patrons weren't really enjoying themselves.

Jeremy was quick to sense her reservation. "Don't you like this place?" he asked, after they were seated at a banquette against the wall.

"It gets marvelous reviews," she answered quickly.

"But you would have preferred someplace else. I should have asked where you wanted to go," he said penitently.

"This is fine, really. What makes you think I'm not pleased?"

He smiled. "You have a very expressive face."

She sighed, giving up the pretense. "It's been a curse since childhood. I used to make up the most wonderful excuses, but no one ever believed me."

"You don't have to make up stories for me. Tell me what restaurants you like, so I won't make the same mistake next time."

"The food is very good here," she insisted. "It's just that the atmosphere is so...restrained."

"You mean stuffy." He laughed.

"That's not all bad. At least you don't have to worry about getting hit by a flying bread stick."

"My little Pollyanna," he said fondly. "You find a little good in everything—even me."

"You're not so bad for a banker. Clara had difficulty believing you truly *are* one."

"What did she think I was?" he asked casually.

"Something shady, although she wasn't specific."

Meredith tipped her head to study his well-shaped head and broad shoulders. His tawny eyes gleamed with amusement as he gazed back at her.

"You don't really look like a banker," she proclaimed. "You don't act like one, either."

"How many of our kind have you known intimately?"

"Does anyone ever know a banker intimately?" she asked in disdain.

He grinned. "Is that a rhetorical question, or are you asking for details of my love life?"

"You asked about *my* relations with members of your profession," she said reprovingly. "I never got past a glassy-eyed stare."

"I can see where that would prejudice you. I hope I've convinced you that we do have feelings."

If he was referring to those expert kisses, that was far from proof. They were calculated in the first place, and underneath his apparent passion was a cool control.

"I suppose you're the exception that proves the rule," she said lightly. "You're certainly atypical. You aren't a family man, and your friends are . . . unusual."

"If you're referring to Al, he's a business acquaintance. You've never met my friends."

"What kind of people do you hang out with?" she asked curiously.

He shrugged. "The usual kind."

"Are they married couples? Other bachelors? What?"

"Some are married, some aren't."

"Are you really close to anyone?" Meredith persisted. The few facts they'd exchanged about their backgrounds didn't give a clear picture of the man. Jeremy was still an enigmatic figure. She wanted to know the little ordinary details of his life. If she found out he normally led the same kind of everyday existence as anyone else, maybe he would cease to intrigue her so much.

His expression was shuttered, almost austere. "Most people have a lot of acquaintances but few close friends. I had a very special one."

"Had?" Meredith asked in a muted voice.

"He died tragically."

"I'm sorry," she murmured. "I shouldn't have asked."

He stared at her for a moment without seeing her, lost in a painful past. Then his gaze focused. "You couldn't have known," he answered politely.

After an embarrassing pause, Meredith changed the subject awkwardly. "This veal is delicious."

His glance at her bent head held compassion. "Yes, it's excellent," he said gently.

The brief glimpse Jeremy had given her into his private life wasn't repeated, but neither was his somber mood. He was as charming and urbane as ever. The small chink in his armor was revealing, however. Under that smooth exterior, he was capable of dark passions and deep emotions. It was reassuring and frightening at the same time.

After they'd finished dinner and the plates were cleared away, the waiter presented menus once more.

"May I serve you dessert?" he asked in his best formal manner.

"Just coffee," Jeremy replied without consulting her.

Meredith was surprised, but a moment later she discovered why. Another waiter wheeled over a cart bearing a tremendous birthday cake. The entire rectangle was bordered by lit candles that illuminated an airplane in the center. A small figure clad in a jumpsuit was emerging from the cockpit.

"You were really serious about giving me a party," she exclaimed. "But that cake is so huge!"

"I thought you deserved better than a cupcake with one candle. The festivities have just begun."

"Don't tell me the waiters are going to sing 'Happy Birthday.'" She laughed.

"I wouldn't trust these clowns. It would probably sound like the lament from *Pagliacci*."

At that moment a young woman approached their table holding the strings of a dozen brightly colored balloons. Behind her was a young man dressed in a tuxedo. While she presented the balloons to Meredith, he sang a highly embellished version of "Happy Birthday."

Meredith was slightly dazed, but she wasn't the only one. The whole room watched, openmouthed.

When the young man had finished his enthusiastic rendition, Jeremy stood up. "Ladies and gentlemen, will you all join in singing 'Happy Birthday' to my lovely fiancée, after which I'd like you to share her birthday cake with us."

Meredith was appalled. Everyone would think he was drunk or crazy. They were the kind of people who looked right through strangers. How could she expect them to do something so spontaneous?

A stunned silence greeted Jeremy's invitation, confirming Meredith's fears. She felt achingly sorry for him, but he wasn't the least bit embarrassed. He and the young man started to sing with gusto.

Then an amazing thing happened. People all over the room began to join in, hesitantly at first, then with increasing volume. Even the waiters turned from blank-faced robots into smiling human beings.

Applause and a loud buzz of conversation greeted the end of the song. Jeremy thanked everyone and told Meredith to blow out the candles.

"Now make a wish," he instructed.

She closed her eyes obediently—and wished for things that amazed her. When she opened her eyes, he was gazing at her with an unreadable expression.

"I hope all your wishes come true, sweet Meredith," he said tenderly.

"So do I," she whispered.

The electric moment was broken by a waiter bearing a bottle of champagne. "The guests at that table would like you to have this," he said, indicating a handsome older couple at a nearby table.

They smiled and nodded when Meredith looked over and indicated her thanks. After that, a steady procession of people stopped by to offer congratulations.

"You're a very lucky girl," a dignified matron told Meredith. "If more young men were that romantic, there would be fewer divorces."

"They aren't married yet, Martha," her husband joked.

"Don't be cynical, James. I'm sure their marriage will be one long fairy tale."

Jeremy grinned, taking Meredith's hand. "We're living in one right now."

"Aren't they a darling pair?" another woman who had joined them commented.

The two couples turned aside and started conversing. All over the room people were chatting with one another as though at a party. The sterile atmosphere had changed dramatically.

"I can't believe this," Meredith marveled. "Are these the same people who were here when we came in?"

Jeremy smiled. "I hope you're enjoying your birthday as much as they are."

"Much more," she answered softly. "No one's ever done such a thoughtful thing for me before."

"That's too bad, because you deserve the best." He reached into his pocket. "In all the excitement I almost forgot to give you your present."

She took the small beribboned box uncertainly. "You've already done enough."

"What's a birthday without a gift?"

Inside the gaily wrapped box was an intricately sculpted gold ring. On closer examination, Meredith realized the design was formed by her initials intertwined with Jeremy's.

"I can't take this. It's too expensive," she protested.

"It isn't polite to mention the cost of a gift," he teased.

"I suppose it *will* lend weight to our engagement," she said hesitantly.

"I didn't give it to you for that reason." He slipped the ring on her finger. "I hoped it would be a reminder of me."

"How could I ever forget you?" she asked softly.

They gazed at each other, their lips only a few inches apart. For the first time, Meredith felt that Jeremy's emotion was real. Unfeigned desire smoldered in his eyes as he bent his head toward hers. She parted her lips, staring at his firm mouth, anticipating its feel against hers.

"I was instructed to tell you how delicious the cake was." A smiling waiter stood over them.

Jeremy managed to mask his look of annoyance. "I'm glad everyone enjoyed it."

Meredith felt as frustrated as he, but she realized the interruption had been timely. They'd been drifting toward something they'd both regret. Her involvement with Jeremy was complicated enough without adding a physical dimension.

She was slightly tense when she said good-night, although he had promised not to repeat his previous behavior. The black sedan wasn't in evidence, so there was no reason for him to.

It had followed her during the day, but when Jeremy picked her up, the man was evidently no longer concerned. Last night must have convinced Al they were at least going together. He had apparently instructed his man to keep an eye on her only when she wasn't with Jeremy.

"Thank you for a wonderful evening," she said at her door.

"I'm glad you had a good time," he said pleasantly.

"Everyone did. I still can't get over how those people thawed out like a bunch of melting Popsicles."

"It just goes to show you can never tell what to expect from anyone." His smile was distorted by the shadows on his face.

"I suppose you're right," she answered slowly.

"Good night, honey." He bent his head and kissed her cheek briefly.

It was what she wanted, what she knew to be sensible, but Meredith couldn't help sighing as she got ready for bed.

Chapter Four

Meredith had no trouble feigning delight when she showed Clara her birthday present the next morning.

"It was the most incredible party! Jeremy had all those stuffed shirts acting like human beings," she bubbled.

"That's nice." Clara's mouth looked a little pinched. "At least you had a proper celebration—even if it *was* a month late."

Meredith was belatedly sorry for her thoughtlessness. The older woman's feelings were clearly hurt. "I had a wonderful birthday party with you and Milt," she assured her. "Last night was fun because it was so off the wall, but it didn't compare to being with family."

"We feel as though you belong to us," Clara said slowly. "But maybe we get a little too possessive at times."

"Not true at all. I feel the same way about you two. Some day I hope to have a marriage like yours."

Clara smiled, mollified. "You will if you stop being so picky."

Meredith realized this was her opportunity to set the stage for her bogus engagement announcement. "You'll be happy to hear I think I've struck pay dirt."

Clara's smile faded. "Jeremy Winchester?"

Meredith nodded. "He's very exciting."

"So is a roller coaster, but you wouldn't necessarily want to spend all your time on one."

"Make up your mind," Meredith answered with only half-feigned exasperation. "First you tell me I'm too picky, then you warn me off the first man who's interested me in ages."

"I was simply reminding you that you don't know anything about him," Clara said defensively.

"How can I if I don't go out with him?" Meredith frowned. "It isn't like you to form irrational dislikes before even getting to know a person."

After assessing Meredith's annoyed expression, Clara did an abrupt turnaround. "You're right. We got off to an inauspicious start, but anyone's entitled to a bad day. Why don't you bring Jeremy over for dinner so we can get acquainted with him?"

"That's a good idea," Meredith answered evasively. She wanted Clara to approve of him—but at a distance.

"How about tomorrow night?" the other woman suggested promptly.

"Well, I . . . I don't know what his plans are."

"Why not call and ask him right now?"

"I don't want to disturb him at work. I'll wait and ask him tonight." Meredith brightened as a stall tactic occurred to her. "But I guess that wouldn't give you enough advance notice."

"How long do you think it takes to cook dinner for four people?"

"I was hoping for more than pizza," Meredith teased.

"You'll get it—including crow for dessert. I may be out of practice, but I can still whip up a dandy meal. You'll see. How's dinner at eight?"

"I told you, I'll have to check with Jeremy first."

"If he's busy, come without him. You issued a challenge, and I'm taking you up on it."

Meredith was relieved when Jeremy called that evening, since she didn't know how to get in touch with him. He wasn't listed in the telephone book, and he hadn't given her his number. How would she ever explain that to Clara?

After first thanking him for the birthday party, she told him about Clara's invitation.

"I'm sorry, but I can't make it tomorrow night," he said. "I'm flying up to Tahoe, and I don't know what time I'll get back."

"I assume you're taking a commercial flight. Did my flying scare you?" she joked.

"I'd trust you anytime," he answered warmly.

"Well, then? We could use the business." That wasn't the only reason.

"I want you to stay as far away from Al as possible."

"Are you afraid you can't keep up the appearance of being in love with me?' she asked provocatively, reminding him of his similar accusation.

"That's the easy part." His voice was like liquid honey. "The hard part is forgoing those passionate kisses. Are you sure you won't reconsider?"

"Only in front of Al." She figured that was a safe concession.

He heaved a mock sigh. "You're a cold woman, Miss Collins."

If he only knew! The memory of his firm mouth and ruggedly masculine body was disrupting her pulse rate.

"Not cold, just prudent," she answered hastily. "I don't want you to get carried away by your role."

"You're probably right. It wouldn't be difficult," he murmured.

The suggestive tone of the conversation warned Meredith that they were drifting too close to intimacy. She changed the subject abruptly. "Will your business in Tahoe take all day?"

"It shouldn't but I have to remain flexible. Otherwise I'd be delighted to have dinner with your friends."

"I wasn't asking for that reason. Actually I'm relieved that you can't make it."

"But I intend to," he answered firmly. "Ask them to schedule it for another night."

Meredith bowed to the inevitable, knowing that between Clara and Jeremy, she was fighting a losing battle. "What night would be convenient?" she asked fatalistically.

After they'd made a date and hung up, she realized that she'd again forgotten to ask Jeremy for his phone number. It wasn't urgent, but she made a mental note to ask him next time he called. In case something came up, she should know how to get in touch with him.

Clara wasn't too disconcerted the next morning when Meredith told her Jeremy was busy. "We'll have a nice visit anyway."

"Are you sure you don't want to put dinner in the freezer until Friday night?" Meredith asked. That was the night he had selected.

"I'd have to arm myself with a chair and a whip if I told Milt you weren't coming tonight. He's looking forward to seeing you."

Meredith laughed. "I'd be more flattered if I didn't know how bored he is."

"Better times are coming, glory be! The doctor says he can start going out next week, and resume flying the week after."

"That's great news! I'll stop on the way over tonight and pick up a bottle of champagne to celebrate," Meredith said.

Milt was as happy to see her as Clara had predicted, although he hid his delight under a brusque manner. "It's about time you showed up," he growled. "I suppose broken-down old men don't interest you."

"Not especially." She grinned and kissed his cheek. "Fortunately I don't know any."

"Don't give me any of that blarney. I'm the one who's Irish."

"Then let's see some of that Irish charm, or I'll find a man who appreciates me."

"Clara tells me you already have."

Well, that didn't take long, Meredith thought ruefully. "I'd better go help her get dinner," she said hastily.

"No, stay here and talk to Milt." Clara thwarted her neatly. "I don't want you coming in at the last minute and taking credit for my culinary effort."

Meredith took a seat next to him, stifling a sigh of resignation. "It will certainly be nice to have you back," she remarked, hoping to divert him. She was successful, but only temporarily.

"You haven't really needed me these past weeks," he answered.

"It's the slow season."

"Tell that to the utility companies, among others. They send bills all year round."

"Business will pick up," she assured him, showing more confidence than she felt.

"Have you gotten any encouragement on a loan?"

"You know how bankers are," she answered vaguely. "Glaciers move like greased lightning compared to them."

"Damn these cracked ribs!" Milt pounded the arms of his chair. "I ought to be out knocking some sense into those guys instead of sending you to do a man's job."

"Don't be such a male chauvinist. Bankers are preponderantly men, and I'm prettier than you."

His response wasn't equally lighthearted. "I want this loan as much as you do, Meredith, but not at any price."

She returned his gaze steadily. "I'm going to pretend you didn't say that, Milt."

His eyes wavered. "I'm sorry. It's just that Clara said your new boyfriend is a banker, and I didn't want . . . that is, we talked it over. . . ." His voice trailed off.

"You two haven't had much time for television lately, have you?" she asked with grim amusement.

"You know how we feel about you, Merry," he said awkwardly.

The small endearment told her more than words. Milt was fiercely sentimental, but he would have denied it vehemently.

"Don't worry," she said fondly. "A helicopter won't buy my affections. Now, a jumbo jet might be another matter."

"What would you do with it?" he asked gruffly, to hide his relief and embarrassment. "That's the one thing you can't fly."

"You're right. Scratch the jumbo jet, too."

Clara announced dinner, and Meredith hoped the subject of Jeremy had been put to rest. She was mistaken, although things started out well. They toasted Milt's imminent return to health, and Meredith praised Clara's cooking.

"These dumplings are light as a feather," she marveled. "You really do know how to cook."

"They didn't have take-out food when we were first married." Milt grinned. "Today's brides don't even have to own a can opener."

"They don't know what a can opener is," Clara commented. "Nowadays everything comes out of the deep freeze, and goes into the microwave oven."

"Think of all the time that saves," Meredith pointed out.

"I suppose so, but I really enjoyed cooking dinner from scratch tonight," Clara replied. "I'd almost forgotten that a chicken is born with more parts than thighs, legs and breasts. That's the way they're packaged in the supermarket. Today's children are bound to grow up confused."

"Only if they're called on to assemble one." Meredith helped herself to another portion. "This is great!"

"A real treat," Milt agreed. "Merry's boyfriend doesn't know what he missed."

"Maybe I'll have steak Friday night," Clara remarked thoughtfully. "That's always a safe bet with men. What do you think, Meredith?"

"It sounds fine," she answered tepidly.

"I'm looking forward to meeting this fellow," Milt said. "What's he like?"

"He's very nice," she said.

"That's not much of a description," Milt complained.

"You'll see for yourself when he gets here."

"I wasn't asking what he looks like," he persisted. "I want to know what kind of person he is."

"You can decide that for yourself, too."

"Are you being purposely noncommittal, or don't you know anything about him, either?" Milt asked shrewdly.

Meredith sighed. "I can see Clara's been airing her views."

"Well, you must admit you're being somewhat secretive."

"Because I'd rather discuss more interesting topics than the new men in my life?" Meredith asked defensively.

"See? She said men—plural." Milt sent his wife a triumphant look. "I told you it wasn't anything serious. You're getting all upset over nothing."

She stared at him in disgust. "Take my advice, Milt. If anyone ever offers you a diplomatic post, turn it down."

"What's the point in beating around the bush?" he demanded. "When you want to find out something, you ask. You've been stewing over this thing for no good reason. Meredith is dating the guy, but she isn't serious about him. It's as simple as that."

Meredith wasn't at all happy with the developments. Milt wasn't the only one who wasn't cut out for intrigue, she decided wryly. How could she put their minds at rest and still set the stage for a romance between herself and Jeremy? Al had ingenious methods of collecting information. If she didn't correct Milt's impression, either he or Clara could give the game away.

"I didn't say I wasn't serious about Jeremy," she said carefully. "He's a tremendously stimulating man."

Milt frowned. "What's that supposed to mean?"

"You *are* getting old," Clara murmured.

Meredith felt hot color flood her cheeks. "I enjoy being with him," she said hastily.

"So you have a good time together. That's no basis for deciding you're in love with the guy," Milt objected.

"It's a step in the right direction," she said.

"You just met. What do you really know about each other?"

"You can analyze any relationship out of existence," Meredith replied impatiently.

"I'm not trying to get into a debate with you," Milt said. "I'm simply advising you to keep things in perspective. You met a handsome man and you like going out with him. There's nothing wrong in that."

"Well, at least we agree on one thing," Meredith commented ironically.

"Right. Just tell Clara that's all it is, so she'll stop worrying that you're getting involved with a shady character."

Clara shot Meredith a worried look. "Milt, I didn't say—"

"Meredith knows you have only her best interests at heart." He overrode his wife's protest.

"I appreciate your concern, but I resent the implication that I'm not bright enough to make my own decisions," Meredith remarked coolly.

"Jeremy is handsome enough to cloud any woman's judgment," Clara said placatingly.

"He's scarcely the first good-looking man I've ever gone out with."

"No, but there's something . . . special about him."

"I rest my case," Meredith said with satisfaction.

"Maybe he's everything you think he is. I sincerely hope so," Clara said earnestly. "Milt and I would simply like to know more about him. Is that so reprehensible?"

"I guess not," Meredith admitted grudgingly.

Milt had been restraining himself with an effort. "What's his background? Where does he come from?"

"If he's not a native San Franciscan, I imagine he's lived here for quite a few years," Meredith answered.

"You don't know?"

"Well, no, it never came up, but it stands to reason. He has a beautiful home, and he's president of a bank."

"Does he belong to any clubs or organizations in the city?"

"How on earth would I know? I haven't known him long enough to find out things like that."

"Exactly. How about his friends? Have you met any of them?"

"We...there hasn't been time yet."

"So you don't have any proof that he's anything he says he is."

"Stop browbeating the girl," Clara intervened unexpectedly. "She isn't on trial, for heaven's sake!"

Milt gave his wife an outraged look. "You were the one who started all this. *You* said she was getting too chummy with a guy who didn't seem on the up-and-up. Then when I try to find out if you're right, all of a sudden I'm the heavy!"

"You don't have to give her the third degree," Clara said impatiently. "Can't you ever discuss things calmly? Why do you always have to go after a gnat with an elephant gun?"

Meredith stared at the older couple without really seeing them. It had suddenly occurred to her that Milt might be right. What proof did she have that the few things Jeremy had told her about himself were the truth? She'd never met anyone who knew him—except Al, who wasn't much of a character witness. Jeremy had never offered her his unlisted phone number, nor invited her to visit his bank. She'd simply taken everything he told her on faith. How did she even know he was a banker? And if he'd lied about that, she'd gotten herself into an unholy mess!

"Meredith?" Clara was looking at her with a puzzled frown.

Meredith realized that Clara must have been trying to get her attention. She managed a weak smile. "I was waiting until you got through yelling at each other instead of me."

"There won't be any more yelling going on," Clara stated firmly. "Will there, Milt?"

He grinned sheepishly. "Sorry about that, Merry. I guess I got a little carried away."

"That's okay." She smiled. "You convinced me not to take up a life of crime, anyway. I'd be rotten on a witness stand."

"Maybe it's just as well he got it out of his system before Friday night," Clara said.

Meredith's smile faded. "Perhaps we should reconsider about Friday night. There isn't any real hurry. We can do it another time."

"Now see what you've done!" Clara scolded her husband. "She doesn't want you within a mile of her boyfriend, and I can't say I blame her."

Milt looked aggrieved. "I said I was sorry. What more can I do?"

"You can promise not to grill him like a hamburger."

"Milt has been speaking his mind for fifty-four years, and we both know he's not about to change," Meredith intervened. "It would be a very uncomfortable evening, so I'd like to propose an alternative. Let me find out more about Jeremy, and then I'll be able to answer your questions."

After a glance at his wife's pursed mouth Milt said, "If you don't want to see a long happy marriage fall apart, you'll bring your young man over for dinner." He gave Meredith a sudden elfin grin. "Please, Merry, I'm too old to be a swinging single."

"At least you got that one right," Clara said grimly. "I wish you'd reconsider, Meredith. I'll see that Milt behaves himself."

Meredith smiled ruefully. "That's like promising it won't snow in Alaska next winter. It's theoretically possible, though highly unlikely. But Jeremy and I will be here on Friday. I wouldn't want to be responsible for a divorce."

"Thanks, I owe you one," Milt said. "Now can I have my dessert?" he asked Clara.

Meredith usually enjoyed the O'Malleys' company, but that night she was distracted. Pretending fatigue from her late nights with Jeremy, she left early without arousing their suspicions.

Her own suspicions were running rampant, however. The doubts Milt had planted in her mind sprouted like poisonous weeds. Was the story Jeremy told her true? He was certainly spending a lot of time and money to back it up. Whatever his game was, the stakes were high.

Meredith turned over in bed and punched the pillow impatiently. Why shouldn't she believe him? He'd explained everything logically. Al was the sole reason for all the intrigue. And after their meeting in Tahoe, she could well believe Al was paranoid. It was perfectly understandable that Al would call off a deal if he suspected a leak. And everyone knew that banks would move mountains to make money...if Jeremy was really a banker— everything hinged on that one point. Fortunately it was something she could find out easily.

* * *

Meredith was up early the next morning, which made the time until the banks opened seem even longer. Her nerves were vibrating when finally she was able to dial Jeremy's number.

"Northern Pacific Savings and Loan, may I help you?" a professionally cheerful voice asked.

"I..." Meredith had to pause to clear her throat. "May I speak to Jeremy Winchester, please?"

"Who shall I say is calling?" the woman asked.

"Meredith Collins," she answered automatically.

As tremendous relief flooded through her, she regretted giving her name. All she'd wanted was confirmation that he actually worked there. She didn't really want to talk to him in her present state. Why hadn't she simply made some excuse and hung up? But it was too late now.

"Mr. Winchester's office," a carefully modulated voice said.

"I...this is Meredith Collins," she repeated. "I wanted to talk to Mr. Winchester, but if he's busy, I can call back."

"Just a moment, I'll find out."

Jeremy came on the line before Meredith could decide what to say to him. "What a nice surprise. To what do I owe this pleasure?" he asked.

"Well, I...uh..." Her mind went completely blank. She searched desperately for a reason for the call. "I wanted to thank you for the lovely birthday party," she said finally.

"You already did that," he reminded her.

"Did I? Well, I thought it deserved saying again," she answered awkwardly.

"I'm glad you enjoyed the evening." His acknowledgment was somewhat detached.

"I'm sure you're busy, so I won't keep you," she said hurriedly.

"I do have someone in the office right now. Can I call you tonight?"

"That would be fine," she assured him, happy to cut the conversation short.

Jeremy's eyes were thoughtful as he hung up the receiver. "That was strange," he remarked.

"Who was it?" The athletic young man lounging in a chair straightened up instantly.

"Meredith," Jeremy answered tersely.

"What did she want?"

"Nothing. That's what's so strange."

"She must have wanted something. What did she say?"

"She thanked me for a birthday party I gave her a couple of nights ago."

The other man relaxed. "So she has good manners. What's wrong with that?"

"She already thanked me," Jeremy answered succinctly.

"I'm all for caution, but don't you think you're running a little scared?"

"I've gotten to know her, Steve. She has something else on her mind."

"Like what?"

"I don't know. That's what bothers me."

"You cut her off pretty short."

"No, she was the one who was anxious to get away." Jeremy thrust his hands in his pockets, tightening the fabric over his muscular thighs. "Why would she call when she didn't want to talk?"

"Maybe she was checking to see if you came to work today."

"Of course!" Jeremy stopped pacing. "But not just today. She wanted to find out if I told her the truth about my job here."

Steve frowned. "That's not good. It means she still has reservations. I thought you said she bought the whole package."

"I thought she did. Something must have come up to shake her confidence."

"I suppose you realize she's the loose cannon in this operation."

Jeremy ran his fingers through his thick dark hair. "What do you want me to do about it?"

Steve looked pensive. "I don't suppose there's any way we could get rid of her without suspicion?"

"No, she's in business with an older couple who regard her as a daughter. I gather she also has a lot of other friends. We couldn't make her disappear quietly, no matter how inventive we were."

"Too bad. Well, that only leaves one alternative. You'll have to romance her."

"What would that accomplish?" Jeremy demanded.

"If she's in love with you she'll go along with anything you say. And most importantly—she won't ask questions."

Jeremy scowled, resuming his pacing. "You're asking a hell of a lot."

"As I remember, you were the one who offered to do anything."

"I didn't expect that to include innocent people getting hurt," Jeremy muttered.

"What's the big deal? She'll have a great time out of it, and then you make sure to let her down easily. Doesn't the reward justify the means?"

Jeremy's features sharpened into a graven mask. "Yes," he answered in a tone that was almost a snarl.

"All right then. Go to work."

Meredith's phone rang often that night, but Jeremy was the only one she wanted to hear from. She was uncharacteristically diffident when he finally called.

"I hope I didn't disturb you this morning," she said softly.

"My day went downhill from that point on," he replied.

She laughed breathlessly. "Were you refusing some poor wretch a loan?"

"No, I was demanding collateral for a Seeing Eye dog."

"You bankers are all heart."

"Only with beautiful women." His voice deepened. "I missed you last night."

"What time did you get back?" she asked, hiding her pleasure.

"Around midnight."

"Were you with Al all that time?" Meredith exclaimed. "There must be an easier way to make a living."

"I was working on it, but the cards didn't cooperate."

"You were gambling? I thought this was a business trip."

"It was, but I figured I deserved some recreation afterward."

"I never could understand the fascination gambling holds when most of the time people end up losing."

"Ah, but there's always that chance of winning big."

"Everybody knows the odds are against it. How can otherwise sensible people keep going back for more punishment? I've flown enough of them to the casinos. They talk about how much they lost last time, but they still can't wait to get back to the tables."

"Odd, isn't it? People are often pessimistic about their health, their jobs, their marriages, yet they have supreme faith in their ability to control a pair of dice or a deck of cards."

Something in his voice, some underlying intensity, disturbed Meredith. "Is that the way you feel?" she asked slowly.

"No, I just gamble for the fun of it." He changed the subject. "What did you do last night?"

"I went to Clara and Milt's for dinner, which is something I have to talk to you about."

"Are we on for Friday night?"

"Unfortunately, yes. I tried to get out of it, but I couldn't."

"Why would you do that?" he asked. "I told you I wanted to meet them."

"And I was right about it being a rotten idea. You have no idea of what you're in for. Prosecuting attorneys could take lessons from Milt!"

"I don't mind answering a few questions."

"A few! By the time he's through with you, Milt will know more about you than your mother does."

"If it doesn't bother me, why does it bother you?" he asked.

"You forget, I'm part of this charade, and I don't lie well. We're supposed to be attracted to each other."

"Is that a lie, Meredith?" he asked quietly.

She couldn't very well deny the fact. Jeremy was much too experienced with women. He'd felt the quiver that ran through her when their bodies touched. She hadn't struggled very strenuously when he kissed her, either.

"You can be quite charming when you want to," she said carefully.

"So can your mailman, I'm sure, but that wasn't what I meant. I think you know that."

"It isn't uncommon for a man and a woman to be sexually attracted to each other even though they have nothing in common," she replied defensively.

Jeremy chuckled. "I'd say that was a pretty strong common bond."

"That's because you're a man."

"Women aren't interested in sex?"

"It isn't all they look for in a relationship," she answered coolly.

"Men either. I can't say I didn't notice your considerable physical attributes, but the first thing that impressed me was your grace under pressure."

Meredith was inordinately pleased. "I felt the same way about you," she admitted.

"So you see, we have a lot going for us."

"It wouldn't be difficult to pretend we were friends, but we're supposed to be, well . . . more."

"Lovers?" he asked softly.

"Good Lord, no! The O'Malleys don't even want me to date you."

"I plan to change their minds Friday night."

Meredith sighed. "It would be a lot less painful if you could just manage to break your leg between now and then."

"I tried that once when I went skiing. It wasn't what it's cracked up to be, if you'll excuse the pun."

"Okay, but don't say I didn't warn you."

"I'm looking forward to the evening. What time shall I pick you up?"

"I'll have to check with Clara. She works all day at the charter office, so dinner won't be early. She'll have to prepare it after she gets home."

"That seems like an imposition. Why don't I take everybody out to dinner instead?"

"Milt wouldn't be very comfortable in a restaurant. He needs a pillow behind his back when he sits at the table."

"Then I have another idea. Let's have dinner at my house."

"Who would cook it?" Meredith asked warily.

Jeremy laughed. "Don't sound so panicky. I'm not asking you to volunteer. My housekeeper is back from her vacation."

"I wasn't panicky," she said defensively. "It's merely that cooking isn't one of my strong points."

"You have others that make up for it," he said warmly. "Shall I tell Helga to prepare dinner?"

"That might be a good idea. Milt can scarcely act up if he's a guest in your home."

Jeremy chuckled. "From the picture you've drawn, I doubt if that will stop him."

"At least it might slow him down."

"Let me worry about Milt," Jeremy advised. "You can concentrate on looking at me adoringly."

"They'd never believe it," Meredith objected. "It's too out of character."

"That's the way women in love are supposed to act."

"You've made my point."

"I know, I know. You aren't in love with me, and you're not a convincing liar. Well, that only leaves me one course of action."

"What's that?"

"I'll have to make you fall in love with me," he answered softly.

Jeremy's words echoed in her ears long after their conversation ended. He had been joking, of course, but she didn't like the hint of ruthlessness in his voice. He was determined to be convincing Friday night, no matter what it took. The prospect was slightly daunting, since she knew by experience how devastatingly seductive he could be. She could only hope he'd honor his promise to restrain himself.

Jeremy had offered to call for Meredith and the O'Malleys, but she told him that would be foolish. He'd have to make a round trip over the Golden Gate Bridge and back, then repeat the process at the end of the evening.

It made more sense for her to bring the older couple, since they lived in the same suburb. But on the way to their house she had second thoughts. The black sedan was following at a discreet distance, an unwelcome surprise.

Meredith had accepted the man's presence during the day, but she had thought her nights would continue to be unsupervised. Evidently this would be so only when she was with Jeremy—and her shadow couldn't know she was going to meet him. If she'd realized that, she would have let Jeremy call for her. Instead, she was leading the man straight to Clara and Milt.

Meredith's mouth set in a thin line as she imagined the dossier Al was assembling on her. Not that her life couldn't bear scrutiny; it was the indignity that bothered her. Plus the creepy feeling of having her privacy invaded.

The situation afforded a certain amount of grim amusement, however. Tailing her wasn't exactly a glamorous assignment. So far the man had been privileged to visit such exotic places as the dry cleaner's, the post office and the drugstore. Maybe she should spice up his report by dropping in at one of the male strip joints on Broadway, Meredith reflected sardonically. Her smile faded as she remembered they weren't playing a game.

Clara and Milt were ready and waiting—one with more enthusiasm than the other.

"You'd think we were visiting the Pope," Milt grumbled. "Clara supervised every article of my clothing except my shorts."

"If I hadn't, you'd probably have worn a jogging suit," she commented.

"I'm a sick man. I'm entitled to be comfortable."

"People have had open heart surgery without complaining as much as you do," she answered callously. "Besides, the doctor says you're practically well."

"Sure! Because I told him I wouldn't pay his bill if he didn't let me out of this damn house," Milt muttered.

"You change sides oftener than a Ping-Pong ball. Will you make up your mind whether you want to be treated like a sick person or a well one?"

"We're going to be late," Meredith intervened. "Would you mind finishing this argument in the car?"

Milt winked at her. "I hope you have a full tank of gas. It's been going on for twenty-five years."

Chapter Five

Meredith could tell that Clara and Milt were impressed by their first glimpse of Jeremy's home. As she swung in to the curb, she also noticed that the black sedan continued down the street and turned the corner. She was now safely in Jeremy's custody. Had he agreed to the arrangement? No, that couldn't be. He would have told the man he needn't follow her, since she would be coming to his house.

Meredith was suddenly impatient with herself. When was she going to stop being suspicious of Jeremy? Everything he'd told her checked out. It was all the O'Malleys' fault. She hoped Jeremy could pull things off tonight so they'd stop bugging her.

He opened the door wearing his most charming smile. After the introductions had been made he showed them into the living room, which looked less formal than the first time Meredith had seen it. All the lamps were lit, and an inviting fire crackled in the black marble fireplace. Two love seats were placed at right angles to the hearth. A round coffee table held a tray of assorted cheeses and crackers.

While they seated themselves by the fire, Jeremy moved to a well-stocked bar cart nearby.

"What can I get everyone to drink?" he asked. "Scotch? Bourbon? Gin? I also have an assortment of wines and liqueurs if anyone would like something less potent."

"That's quite an impressive display," Milt remarked. "You must take your drinking seriously." The bland expression on his face indicated his observation was a joke, but nobody was fooled.

So much for Milt's promise to behave himself, Meredith thought grimly. Clara was equally annoyed. She glared balefully at her husband, while Jeremy merely looked amused.

"Liquor is way down the list of my priorities," he answered Milt's comment smoothly. "But I do enjoy a drink before dinner with friends. I can get you a plain soda water, though, if you have some prejudice against alcohol."

"I don't believe in being prejudiced," Milt replied swiftly. "Make mine a Scotch on the rocks."

A pleasant-looking older woman in a black uniform came into the room with a plate of hot hors d'oeuvres.

"This is Helga," Jeremy said. "The best cook in San Francisco."

As the woman smiled her gratification, Milt stared deliberately at Jeremy's flat midsection. "You must not eat at home very much, then. But I suppose it's normal for a bachelor to be out every night with a different girl. Ah, to be young again." He heaved an exaggerated sigh.

"You won't get much older if you keep this up," Clara muttered.

He gave Jeremy a conspiratorial wink. "Women like to picture single men as poor lonely souls who never have any fun."

"The notion that we're out every night with a different woman is equally misleading," Jeremy said. "At least in my case." He gave Meredith a meaningful look. "Especially since I met this beautiful lady."

"How long has it been now?" Milt asked. "Two or three days?"

"A little over two weeks," Jeremy corrected him.

It *was* that long since she'd flown him to Tahoe, although they hadn't seen each other again until more than a week later. She decided to step in before Milt thought to ask how many dates they'd had.

"It seems like so much longer," she said softly, gazing at Jeremy with shy delight. "Jeremy and I feel as though we've known each other all our lives."

She was afraid she'd overdone it when Clara looked at her in mild amazement, but Jeremy followed her lead deftly.

"I wish we *had* known each other always. Meredith must have been an enchanting child," he remarked to the O'Malleys.

"She was." Clara, at least, was diverted. Her face was soft with remembrance. "We loved looking after her when her parents were away."

"Distance certainly lends enchantment." Meredith laughed. "You evidently don't remember the time I dumped your prized bottle of Shalimar perfume into the goldfish bowl so the fish would smell better."

Clara smiled. "Sometimes we enjoyed having you better than other times."

"And here I thought you were perfect," Jeremy teased Meredith.

"I'll bet you did worse things," she challenged.

"Depends on how you look at it," he said. "I broke a few windows playing baseball. But those were accidents."

"Where does a city kid play baseball?" Milt asked. "You must have grown up somewhere else."

"No, I've lived in this house almost all my life. We played in the backyard—that's how the windows got broken. Skinny Wainwright and I went without an allowance for one whole summer." Jeremy chuckled. "He was my best friend and neighbor."

"You still live at home with your parents?" Milt asked incredulously.

"Only when they come to visit. They moved to Arizona years ago."

"Don't you find this place awfully big for one person?" Clara asked.

"I suppose it is, but I'm used to having a lot of space. I wouldn't be happy in an apartment. Besides, it won't be too big when I get married." He smiled at Meredith.

"You mean *if* you get married, don't you?" Milt asked bluntly. "You've avoided taking the plunge so far—at least I'm assuming you have. I wouldn't say you were much of a candidate."

Jeremy put his arm around Meredith. "Don't you think it's time we told them?" he asked.

She stiffened automatically, unwilling to bring the deception into the open. "Well, we haven't exactly..."

"I didn't mean to jump the gun, angel." He ruffled her hair fondly. "I just thought we ought to set Milt's mind at rest. He seems to think I'm a latter-day Casanova."

"What are you trying to say?" Milt zeroed in on the part he considered important.

"We're engaged," Jeremy told him when Meredith didn't answer.

"Is that true?" Milt asked her.

She hadn't realized how difficult it would be to lie to Clara and Milt. But as Jeremy's arm tightened warningly around her shoulders she said, "Yes, it's true."

"You don't seem very damn happy about it." Milt scowled.

"I am!" Her glance at Jeremy was adoring, if a little belated. "We're both riding on a fluffy white cloud, aren't we, darling?"

"Those fluffy white clouds are the ones that cause turbulence," Milt observed cynically. "You ought to know that."

"I thought you'd be happy for us," she said in a hurt voice.

"We are," Clara answered for him hastily. "It seems so sudden, though. That's all Milt was trying to say."

"Jeremy believes in love at first sight, and I've come to agree with him."

"You must have been trying to conceal the fact from me," Clara commented with raised eyebrows. "I got the impression that you disliked each other rather intensely."

Jeremy laughed. "You'll have to admit we weren't indifferent."

"We did get off on the wrong foot," Meredith said. "But we discovered each other a few hours later. I never told you how much help Jeremy was in that dreadful storm because I didn't want to worry you, but we might not have made it if he hadn't been there to monitor the instrument panel for me." That might not have been strictly true, but she had a feeling it would impress Milt.

It did. His frown lessened. "You're a pilot?" he asked Jeremy.

"No, that's what made his performance so impressive." Meredith pressed her advantage. "He'd never been in a cockpit, but he followed instructions and helped me keep the plane on course."

"That was a pretty bad storm," Milt conceded. "We're in your debt for that one."

"Meredith was the impressive one," Jeremy said. He looked deeply into her eyes. "I realized then I wanted to keep on entrusting my life to her."

She gazed back at him wistfully, wishing for a fleeting moment that he meant it. They'd reached a rare moment of rapport that night. If only their relationship could have grown normally. But Jeremy wasn't an ordinary man, and their situation was a sham. She mustn't allow herself to get so caught up in his mystique that she forgot those things.

"That's very romantic, but did you ever stop to think that being in a dangerous situation together might have colored your thinking?" Milt asked, mildly for him.

"I didn't look for reasons, I only knew I loved her," Jeremy answered simply.

Clara broke the small silence that fell. "If Meredith feels the same way, we're happy for you, of course."

"Jeremy has changed my life. I've never known anyone like him," she said truthfully.

"I'm an outspoken man," Milt said slowly. "I can't pretend I approve. You seem to be a nice enough fellow, Jeremy, but I think you two should get to know each other better before you make such an important decision."

"We aren't planning on getting married right away," Meredith said hastily.

"Well, that's sensible." Milt looked relieved.

"I'm not taking her away from you," Jeremy said gently. "She'll always be part of your life. I'm just asking you to share her with me."

"You're a nice person, Jeremy." Clara's voice had a catch in it.

Meredith suddenly felt awful. She stood up abruptly, mumbling, "I need some ice."

"I'll get it for you." Jeremy followed her to the bar cart.

She looked up at him miserably. "I can't go through with it," she whispered.

"Will you excuse us for a moment?" he asked the other couple.

Clara nodded indulgently, realizing—for the wrong reason—that they wanted to be alone.

When they reached the entry Meredith said, "I can't go on lying to them."

"You have to!" He gripped her shoulders urgently. "We've gone too far to back out now."

"You're asking me to make my dearest friends miserable simply to keep Al happy. Well, I won't do it! If he's stupid enough to back out of your deal just because I know about it, that's tough."

"It's gone way beyond that now. Don't you see? We went to great lengths to convince him that we're involved. You can bet his man reported back to him on that. How do you think Al will react to the news that it was all an act?"

"He'll blow his stack and tell you to get lost, but so what? Your bank won't go under if you lose this deal."

"You're not thinking clearly," Jeremy said impatiently. "What if he thought you deceived me, too? That you're in on some kind of plot against him?"

She stared at him in horror. "You'd let him believe that?"

"Of course not! But Al doesn't trust anything people tell him. He makes up his own mind, and he can be very vindictive if he thinks he's been crossed. It's your welfare I'm concerned about." He paused. "And the O'Malleys'."

Meredith's eyes widened. "They never even heard of him!"

"Would you be convinced if you were Al? They're your partners."

"My God, what have I gotten them into?" she whispered.

"Nothing," he answered swiftly. "They'll be fine, and you will, too. As long as we keep to our original plan. The whole thing will be over with before you know it."

"Sure," she said bitterly. "You and Al will make millions, and Clara and Milt will be heartbroken."

Jeremy grinned unexpectedly. "A broken engagement won't devastate them. They're not that crazy about me."

"You were gaining ground," she said ruefully. "Maybe you'd better say something outrageous."

"Like what?"

"I don't know. You're the one who got us into this mess. It's up to you to get us out."

"I will, honey." He drew her close and guided her head to his shoulder. "Trust me. Everything's going to work out."

She allowed herself the luxury of relaxing in his arms for a moment. Their mild deception had turned into a dangerous game. Al was a sinister figure, and there could be unexpected pitfalls ahead. But Jeremy's big sinewy body inspired confidence. When he held her close, she felt nothing bad could possibly happen to her.

A discreet cough made them aware of the house-keeper's presence. "Dinner is ready when you are, Mr. Winchester," Helga said.

The dining room was softly lit by candles on the polished fruitwood table and in sconces on the wall. They flickered on the crystal wineglasses and illuminated the centerpiece of ruby-red roses. Embroidered white linen place mats were set with sterling flatware and crimson and gold service plates.

When they were seated, Milt surveyed the elegant table. "I see you brought out the company dishes for us."

Clara lifted her eyes to the ceiling. "Dear Lord, I can't take him anywhere!"

Jeremy laughed. "He's perfectly right. I was trying to impress you."

"You succeeded," Clara assured him. "The table is lovely."

Milt grinned. "I'll never hear the end of this when we get home."

"At least you know what to expect," she answered stonily.

"Do you have dinner like this every night?" Milt asked Jeremy. "When you eat at home, that is."

"No way. I often have a tray in front of the television in the den."

"That's my point," Milt said to his wife. "The man has gone to a lot of trouble for us. The least we can do is acknowledge the fact."

Meredith smiled. "He does have a point."

Helga brought in the first course, sautéed mushrooms on thin wedges of buttery toast. They were cooked to perfection, tasting even better than they looked.

"This is marvelous, Helga," Meredith exclaimed after the first bite. "And the hot hors d'oeuvres were outstanding."

"I'm glad you enjoyed them, Miss Collins." The woman smiled.

"For someone who appreciates good food, it's amazing that Meredith never learned how to cook," Clara remarked. "I hope you warned Jeremy about that."

The look he gave Meredith was purely male. "She has other attributes," he murmured.

"Fortunately, because she's a walking disaster in the kitchen," Milt said. "We don't even let her warm up the take-out food."

"One burned pizza and you hear about it for the rest of your life," Meredith grumbled.

The appetizer was followed by a salad of avocado, marinated artichoke hearts and tiny bay shrimp in a vinaigrette dressing. The main course was rare roast beef with Yorkshire pudding and fresh baby peas. By the time the chocolate soufflé cake was served, Milt was in a mellow mood.

"You were right about Helga being the best cook in San Francisco," he said. "I hope you plan on keeping her after you're married."

"Helga has been with the family for many years," Jeremy said without revealing his plans.

Clara had been completely won over. "Do you have any idea when you'll get married?"

Meredith and Jeremy smiled at each other over the predictable question. "Perhaps in the spring," she said vaguely. "Jeremy's unconventional. He wants me to wear a yellow gown and carry a bouquet of daffodils."

Clara looked thoughtful. "That could be very effective. Mimosa blooms in the spring, too. We could decorate the church with it. And what would you think about having the bridesmaids wear pale blue? Of course it's your wedding. I don't mean to be taking over.''

"When the time comes, you can handle everything," Meredith answered noncommittally. "I don't even want to think about it."

Jeremy reached over and covered her clenched fingers with his big warm hand. "You'll be a beautiful bride. Any man would be fortunate to have you."

Clara didn't seem to notice his somewhat ambiguous phrasing. "I'm glad you're not rushing into anything, but I can't help looking forward to the big day." She smiled sentimentally. "I feel like the mother of the bride."

"If you expect me to walk Merry down the aisle, make sure you don't pick opening day of the baseball season." Milt grinned.

"Are you kidding? What could be more important than the opening game?" Jeremy gave the women a mischievous look, going along with the joke.

"Are you a baseball fan?" Milt asked.

"Isn't everyone?" Jeremy answered.

"I met one guy who wasn't, but you wouldn't want to know him. What do you think of the Giants' chances this year?"

As the men started to talk baseball, Clara said softly to Meredith, "Tonight has taught me a lesson. I'll never prejudge anyone again."

"I guess that's always sound policy," Meredith answered vaguely.

"Jeremy is so different than he seemed that first night."

"He has a multifaceted personality," Meredith agreed, a trifle grimly.

"You're not exactly one-dimensional yourself." Clara smiled. "You two will have a very interesting life together."

"If we make it to the altar."

The O'Malleys' complete acceptance of Jeremy was a mixed blessing. It suddenly occurred to Meredith that she'd better prepare Clara for the eventual broken engagement. The older woman wouldn't be as upset if she thought the course of true love was stormy from the beginning.

Clara didn't cooperate, however. She merely looked understanding. "Every woman feels that way after she's made a formal commitment, but you and Jeremy are made for each other. I couldn't have chosen better for you myself."

"You picked Milt, and you've been battling ever since," Meredith teased.

"There are worse things. At least he never bores me."

"That's because you never know what he's apt to say."

"Jeremy isn't predictable, either. He'll keep your life interesting," Clara prophesied.

He already had—in spite of minor traumas. Meredith glanced over at him, noting the animation on his face as he discussed sports. His interests were so varied. She was only beginning to find out how complex he was. How well would she know him by the time this was all over? As she gazed at his cleanly chiseled profile, Meredith felt a little ripple of excitement travel up her spine. Was it apprehension, or anticipation? Or a little of both?

The evening ended in a rosy glow of goodwill. As they prepared to leave, Jeremy kissed Meredith on the cheek.

"You can do better than that," Milt said jocularly.

"As long as I have your permission." Jeremy smiled.

Meredith tensed slightly as he put his hands on her shoulders, but he merely dipped his head and kissed her lightly on the lips.

"We'll wait for you in the car," Milt said. "Come on, Clara, we're inhibiting them."

As the older couple started down the path, Jeremy's arms closed around Meredith's slender figure, and his lips touched hers. She had intended to remain passive, but his seductive mouth called forth a wholly involuntary response. A melting warmth started in her midsection, spreading through her body as it made contact with his. She clung to him, surrendering to the exquisite sensations he was calling forth.

He finally lifted his head and brushed his lips across her cheek. "Thank you, Meredith, for everything," he murmured deeply.

She always found it difficult to orient herself after he'd carried her to the heights. And as usual, his words brought her down swiftly. *Thank you?* Didn't he ever get carried away in the moment? Was every kiss, every caress a calculated act to impress someone? It was a humiliating thought. But this time she rebounded faster.

Drawing away, she said brittlely, "I realize a certain amount of... affection is necessary."

He reached out and smoothed her hair, tucking a shining strand behind her ear. "I wish you felt better about it."

"You're getting what you want," she replied curtly. "Don't push your luck."

Clara and Milt didn't notice how quiet Meredith was on the way home. They were too busy discussing the evening. She dropped them at their house with a feeling of relief. Their praise of Jeremy was almost as difficult to handle as their criticism had been.

The phone rang a few minutes after she entered her apartment. Jeremy's deep voice greeted her, an unwelcome surprise in her present mood.

"If you want to know what Clara and Milt said about you on the way home, you can relax," she said shortly. "They think you're Prince Charming with a modern haircut."

"I'm delighted. I really liked them, but that wasn't why I called."

"To give me my next instructions?" Meredith realized she was acting like a shrew, but disappointment still sat like a weight between her breasts.

"I'm sorry this is such a strain on you. The next couple of days should be easier, though," he consoled her. "You won't have to see me."

"Why not?" His statement didn't bring the relief it should have.

"I'm going out of town. It's my parents' anniversary, and I promised to celebrate with them."

"It came at a fortuitous time, didn't it?" she asked.

His voice was suddenly guarded. "What do you mean?"

"Your...uh...social life has been rather curtailed lately. Without Al's supersnoop hanging around, you can really cut loose. Too bad I can't do the same thing," she remarked lightly.

"I haven't felt deprived. I'm only sorry you do."

He wasn't merely being polite. His voice did hold regret. Did that mean he enjoyed being with her? Or was he remorseful about restricting her life? What, exactly, did Jeremy feel for her?

"I'll survive," she answered finally. Then, against her will, she asked, "When are you coming back?"

"Late Sunday night. Would it make up for your wasted weekend if I brought you a present?"

"Possibly. You can bring me a cactus." It would be a fitting gift—something as thorny as she felt.

After an almost imperceptible pause he said, "You're not allowed to take them out of the state."

"I never heard that," she protested.

"Did you ever hear that it's against the law in Michigan to walk an alligator on the street without a leash?"

"You're making that up."

"If it isn't a law, it should be."

Meredith smiled unwillingly. "Meaning you don't really want to struggle with a spiny cactus."

"I'd rather bring you something romantic, like a lace nightgown the color of moonlight."

"So I could show it to Clara and say you gave it to me?" she asked wistfully.

"No, because I'd like to picture you in it." His voice dropped to a velvet purr.

Meredith's imagination was too vivid for her own good. She too could picture herself in a diaphanous gown, with Jeremy's eyes feasting on all the vulnerable parts of her body through the revealing fabric.

She kept her voice steady with an effort. "You're wasting all that seductiveness. For once we don't have an audience."

"Maybe for once I'm not acting," he answered quietly.

"Maybe?" she asked in a small voice.

He sighed. "It's gotten to be a bad habit, one I hope to kick when this is all over. I hate being devious!"

"You don't have to be with me. We're in this together, remember?"

"How could I forget? You're the only bright spot in my life right now."

It was Meredith's turn to sigh. "You really *can't* be truthful, can you?"

"I am when it counts. One thing you can believe," he said softly. "I'd like very much to make love to you." Before she could respond he said, "Good night, sweet Meredith. Sleep well."

Sleep was the farthest thing from her mind that night. She was plagued by visions of what it would be like if they made love. Jeremy had all the potent masculinity of a Greek god. She'd been close enough to feel the firmness of his torso and the rigidness of his thighs. His naked body would be nothing short of magnificent.

But what kind of lover would he be? From everything she knew about him, he'd be gentle, yet masterful. He would bring ecstasy beyond belief, carrying her to the outer limits of sensation with his impressive power, then fulfilling her completely.

Meredith shuddered and buried her face in the pillow, realizing the extent of Jeremy's hold over her. If all she felt for him was sexual attraction, that would be understandable. He was overpoweringly male. But if she was falling in love with him, *that* could spell disaster. Could you love someone without fully trusting him? She didn't want to face the answer.

Jeremy called Meredith at the charter office on Monday morning. Clara took the call and repeated her thanks for dinner before handing the phone to Meredith.

"Did you have a nice trip?" she asked politely.

"It was all right. It would have been better if you'd been along."

"You didn't ask me."

"Would you have gone?" His voice quickened.

She laughed a little breathlessly. "I might have if I'd known how dull the weekend was going to be."

"Well, at least you missed me," he said dryly. "Even though it was for the wrong reasons."

"This is as good as it gets," she answered cryptically, aware of Clara's presence.

"Does that mean you won't let me make love to you?" he teased.

"Jeremy!" She blushed to the roots of her chestnut hair, remembering her fantasy.

Clara laughed. "I can see I'm in the way. Call me when you're through." She pushed back her chair and went outside.

"It was a valid question," Jeremy was saying.

"At ten o'clock in the morning?"

He chuckled. "What better way to start the day? I can pick you up in half an hour."

"Will you be serious?"

"How do you know I'm not?"

"I don't. I never know what you really mean." Frustration filled her voice.

"You can believe what I said the other night." The teasing note had vanished.

"This isn't the time or the place to discuss it."

"You're right. What are you doing Thursday night?"

Meredith's doubts rushed back. This was only Monday. What was he doing until then? He couldn't want to see her very badly.

"I can't make it Thursday," she said coolly. "A bunch of us are giving a potluck dinner for my best friend, who's getting married."

"Women only?"

"No, there will be couples there," she answered reluctantly.

"Good, I accept with pleasure."

"You won't know anybody."

"I like meeting new people."

"I'm not sure I can go through this whole thing again," she said helplessly.

"The news of our engagement is bound to get around. Don't you think you'll have to answer more questions if I'm *not* with you?"

She sighed. "I suppose so."

"Clara and Milt survived an evening with me," he teased. "How bad an impression can I make on your friends?"

"They'll love you," she answered tonelessly.

"Is that bad? You wouldn't want a wimp for a fiancé."

"Okay, you win—as usual. But don't think it won't cost you. I've been instructed to bring a casserole, which you'll have to eat."

"Is there a chance the O'Malleys were joking the other night about your culinary skills?" he asked.

"If anything, they exaggerated on the plus side."

"In that case, why don't I have Helga whip up a batch of lasagna? Hers is better than any I ever tasted in Italy."

"That would be great if she wouldn't mind."

"No problem, she likes you."

Meredith didn't see or hear from Jeremy until he came to pick her up at eight on Thursday night, the time they'd prearranged. She was extremely annoyed at his casual treatment, but curiosity took precedence when he drew a box out of his pocket and handed it to her.

"What's this?" she asked uncertainly.

"Obviously not a nightgown," he answered mischievously. "It's something to wear under one."

She looked at him blankly. "What do you wear under a nightgown?"

His even white teeth flashed in a grin. "I'm the wrong one to ask. I sleep in the nude."

Meredith's color rose as she added another mental picture to her album—Jeremy sprawled on a big bed, his long arms and legs spread out in relaxation.

She fumbled hurriedly with the beribboned box so she wouldn't have to look at him. Inside was a generous-size bottle of expensive perfume.

"How elegant! This is better than a cactus." Then hurriedly, before he could refer back to the nightgown, she said, "Did you have a good time with your parents?"

"Very nice." Now Jeremy changed the subject. "We'd better go. The lasagna is cooling off in the car."

The party was being held at the home of Evelyn, the friend who had predicted Meredith would be the next bride. Most of the guests were already there when they arrived.

Anyone new was bound to draw attention in the close-knit group, but Meredith was aware of the avid interest Jeremy generated. All of the women, both married and single, eyed him with unconcealed admiration.

Paula admitted to it freely. "You've been holding out on me," she said to Meredith. "Where did you find this ravishing man?"

"You're engaged. You're not supposed to notice other men," her fiancé, Dennis, said good-naturedly.

She laughed. "I'm not comparison shopping, just admiring the view."

Meredith introduced the two men, who shook hands.

"You look familiar," Dennis remarked to Jeremy. "Have we met?"

"I hope not," Meredith said. "Dennis is with the district attorney's office," she explained to Jeremy.

"We do meet some people who aren't criminals," Dennis complained.

"I certainly hope so," Paula said. "Otherwise our dinner parties are apt to be very small."

"I'll only bring home the better class of crooks," he promised. "Some of them are quite charming. Very often you can't distinguish a felon from a law-abiding citizen."

"Come on, you're talking about confidence men. It's their business to be charming." Evelyn's husband, Don, had joined them. "But how about murderers and thieves?"

"The most polished gentleman we ever prosecuted was a hit man for the mob," Dennis said. "He could get a table in a restaurant faster than you could."

"Sure, by killing off the present occupants," Don answered. "That's not class, it's an occupational advantage."

While they were bantering back and forth, a pretty blonde came over and put her hand on Jeremy's arm. "Can I borrow this big strong man for a minute? I need his services," she informed the group.

Jeremy looked at her with amusement. "You'll have to get Meredith's permission."

The blonde fluttered her lashes at him. "To open a jar of olives?"

"I imagine that comes under acceptable behavior." Jeremy chuckled.

Meredith experienced a pang as she watched him walk away with the other woman, smiling down at her with male awareness.

"Cindy was never one for subtlety," Paula sniffed.

"Merry doesn't have to worry," Dennis said loyally. "She has guys standing in line."

"When are you going to make one of them happy and settle down like the rest of us?" Don asked.

It wasn't the ideal time to make the announcement, not with her fiancé drooling over another woman, but Meredith was almost forced into it.

"Well, actually, Jeremy and I are . . . are engaged," she finally managed.

Paula uttered a whoop of joy. "How wonderful!" she exclaimed.

"I'm really happy for you, Merry." Dennis kissed her cheek.

Other people drifted over to see what the excitement was all about, and soon they were surrounded by a group.

"Am I missing something?" Jeremy appeared at Meredith's side.

"I just told everyone our thrilling news," she answered sardonically.

"You'd look happier about a case of the mumps," he murmured.

She had to contain her irritation as Don announced, "This calls for a toast. In case anybody hasn't heard, Meredith and Jeremy are engaged."

While Evelyn brought out champagne, congratulations were offered, and Meredith was forced to smile until her cheeks felt stiff. Her control was sorely tried when Cindy came over and gazed up at Jeremy provocatively.

"You're supposed to congratulate the man, but I think Meredith is the lucky one," she said in a breathy voice.

Jeremy's reply was politely abstracted. His arm was around Meredith, so he could feel the tension in her slight figure. As soon as possible he eased her out of the group and over to a quiet corner of the room.

"Are you okay?" He looked at her with concern. "I didn't realize this was going to make you so unhappy."

"How am I supposed to feel when my fiancé acts like a sex-starved alley cat?" she snapped.

He stared at her blankly. As comprehension dawned, his face relaxed in a smile. "You can't think I was interested in that predatory female?"

"That part doesn't concern me in the slightest," she replied loftily. "I simply think you might have been a bit more discreet."

"How much more discreet could I have been? We were standing in a room full of people."

"Oh, go open another jar of olives," Meredith muttered, trying to brush past him.

Jeremy caught her arms and pulled her against him. "I'm flattered that you're jealous, but—"

"I am *not* jealous!" she flared.

"But," he continued inexorably, "you are a very mixed-up young woman. You're the one I'd like to make love to for a week."

"If you think I'm about to be taken in again by your phony charm, you're crazy!" she stormed.

"I wish you could trust me," he said, gazing down searchingly into her flushed face.

"I don't! You're just using me. I have to go along with you, but I don't have to be happy about it."

"I'm not happy about our situation, either." He traced the shape of her mouth, making the gesture a sensual caress. "I don't want to talk strategy when we're together. I want to tell you how hauntingly beautiful you are. I lie awake nights remembering the perfume of your skin, the tantalizingly chaste touch of your body against mine when we act like lovers in public.''

She resisted the tempting images with an effort. ''That's what you're doing now—acting.''

''No, I'm being completely honest.'' His hands moved up her sides, stopping just short of her swelling breasts.

She grabbed his forearms. ''Jeremy, stop! What will my friends think?''

He chuckled softly, dipping his head and brushing his lips lightly over hers. ''They'll think I'm a very lucky fellow—and I agree.''

''Hey, you two, come back to the party,'' Don called cheerfully. ''You have the rest of your lives to do that.''

Jeremy smiled. ''How long have you been married, Don?''

Jeremy was as big a success with Meredith's friends as he had been with Clara and Milt. As Meredith watched his charm take effect, she was deeply troubled. Would she fall victim to it, too? He always managed to bring her around, no matter how annoyed or downright angry she got at him.

Fear of her own vulnerability made her jumpy as Jeremy walked her to her door at the end of the evening. She jerked nervously when his hand brushed her arm as he reached past her to open the door.

''What's the matter, honey?'' He looked at her quizzically.

''Nothing. I'm just a little tired.''

''Are you sure that's all it is? Or have I done something to upset you?'' he asked quietly.

''No, I'll be fine after I get some sleep,'' she insisted. Then before he could kiss her, even on the cheek, she quickly said, ''Good night, Jeremy.''

He remained on the step, staring at the closed door with narrowed eyes. After a long moment, he turned and walked slowly back to his car.

Chapter Six

After staring at the ceiling for a long time that night, Meredith knew she'd never get to sleep until she worked out her problem. She was falling in love with Jeremy, and she didn't know the extent of his feelings toward her.

That was the reason she kept raising the objection that she couldn't trust him. Jeremy had quieted her fears on that score long ago, but she'd used suspicion as a shield, a safeguard against becoming emotionally entangled. The trouble was, it didn't work anymore. That was evident from the fierce stab of jealousy she'd felt at his interest in Cindy.

Jeremy desired her, that fact was unmistakable. But was anything more than sexual attraction involved? She didn't want a meaningless affair. Should she continue to keep him at arm's length? But that was a coward's way. How could anything ever develop between them if she wasn't willing to take a chance?

Meredith's tense limbs relaxed as she reached a decision. She would stop treating Jeremy as an adversary, and start treating him like a friend. They did enjoy each other's company, and maybe friendship would blossom into something more.

It was fortunate for Meredith's peace of mind that she couldn't follow Jeremy into his bedroom. While he was getting undressed he turned on his telephone answering machine. One of the calls was from Steve, and it sounded urgent: "Call me whenever you get in tonight, no matter how late it is."

Jeremy frowned as he picked up the phone and punched out a number.

Steve answered after one ring. "I've been waiting for your call," he said.

"What's up?" Jeremy asked tersely.

"A couple of things. I'm leaving for the east in the morning, that's why I needed to talk to you tonight. There has been some concern over your gambling. You're getting in over the limit."

"I'm good for it."

"That's not the point," Steve insisted. "You've lost enough. It's time to pull back."

Jeremy smiled mirthlessly. "Maybe I'll win for a change."

"You should know better than that."

"Let me worry about it. Is everything else okay?"

"It is at this end. How are you doing with the girl? Are you making progress?"

Jeremy's frown was back. "I was, but now I'm not so sure. Something happened tonight."

"What?" The other man was instantly alert.

"I don't know, that's what worries me. She's usually so open and straightforward. What could I have done to damage our relationship?" Jeremy sounded almost as though he were talking to himself. "Perhaps I moved too fast."

"You *have* to work fast. We don't have much time. Do you anticipate any problems?"

Jeremy sighed. "No, I hope everything will work out."

"That's not very reassuring," Steve said sharply.

"I'll take care of my part," Jeremy answered irritably. "Just see that you do the same."

Meredith couldn't wait to see Jeremy again and put her new plan into action, but she didn't hear from him. When he didn't phone the office the next day she thought surely he'd call that night. But he didn't. The weekend went by with silence on his part, and she couldn't phone him because the bank was closed.

She could have gone to his house, yet Meredith was reluctant to do that for several reasons. The major one was the fear that she might find him with another woman. He couldn't take anyone else out in public, but he could certainly entertain at home. It was his privilege since their engagement was a sham, but the thought of Jeremy with another woman wasn't a happy one.

Another reason she didn't drop in on him was uncertainty. Maybe he didn't want to see her after the hard time she'd given him at the party. What if any interest he'd felt had waned?

Meredith had no intention of giving up. She might have made things more difficult for herself, but she had one advantage. Jeremy had to keep on seeing her. On Monday morning she called the bank.

"Mr. Winchester is on another line," his secretary said. "Can he call you back?"

"I'll wait," Meredith answered firmly. She wasn't going to sit by the telephone, imagining all sorts of things.

His voice was cordial when he came on the line, relieving some of her fears. "What a delightful surprise," he said.

"Did you have a nice weekend?" she asked, feeling her way.

"So-so. How about you?"

"I worked. Weekends are our only busy times in the winter."

"I suppose they would be," he remarked. "Is business picking up?"

"Not really, but it's always like this."

"That's too bad," he replied vaguely. Jeremy was obviously wondering why she called, but he was too polite to ask.

Meredith knew she couldn't keep him on the phone much longer, so she came to the point. "Could you get away from the bank today?"

"Why? What's wrong?" he asked warily.

"Nothing. I just happen to be at loose ends, and I thought we might do something together. Business is almost nonexistent here on Mondays. Of course I realize a bank is a different matter, but I took a chance . . . I mean, I thought there was a possibility that you might be free."

She ran down finally, aware that she was babbling. But she'd never been in a position of having to ask a man for a date. It was clearly a rotten idea. If Jeremy had wanted to see her, he would have initiated something himself. He seemed to be struggling to find a kind way of declining.

After a moment of silence he said, "You want to see me today?"

"It was just a sudden aberration," she answered hastily. "Everyone I know works for someone else. I thought since you were the boss you could play hooky. But it was a dumb idea. I'll see you around." She was anxious to get off the phone after having made a fool of herself.

"Meredith, wait! You've just had the greatest idea since the invention of scissors. Where do you want to go?"

"Are you sure you don't have anything important to do?" she asked doubtfully, afraid that he'd felt pressured.

"I can always repossess cars tomorrow," he teased. "I do have a couple of things to take care of, though. Is it all right if I don't pick you up until one?"

"That would be perfect!" Her spirits shot up like a skyrocket. "How would you like to drive up to Muir Woods?"

"Sounds great. I'll see you shortly."

Jeremy was a little late getting to Meredith's because he'd gone home to change clothes first. He looked different in a royal-blue jogging suit instead of one of his elegantly tailored business suits, but just as devastatingly handsome. The casual outfit showed off his rangy, athletic body admirably.

She commented on the fact obliquely. "You look very sporty. I've never seen you without a jacket and tie."

"This is an unexpected treat on a Monday—casual clothes and a date with a beautiful woman."

She passed lightly over the compliment. "I'm so glad you could get away. I didn't relish spending the day with the goon in the black sedan."

"I saw his car parked down the block," Jeremy said soberly.

"Do you think he intends to keep this up until your deal is finalized?"

"It looks that way."

"But it's so stupid! He ought to know by now that I don't do anything worth watching. He must be bored out of his skull."

Jeremy smiled. "I can think of worse things than following you around all day. You're a very sexy lady."

"In this?" She was wearing jeans and a bulky white fisherman's sweater over a silk shirt.

An amber glow warmed his eyes. "In anything—or nothing."

"Everyone's sexy in the nude," she commented lightly.

His gaze was penetrating, as though he could see the peaks and valleys hidden under layers of clothing. "You're more enticing fully dressed than a roomful of naked women. The mind boggles at what you're like in the nude."

He didn't make a move toward her. There was even a gently teasing note in his voice, but Meredith's whole body heated. She pretended he was joking, to cover her nervousness.

"I wouldn't want your mind to boggle. It sounds uncomfortable, so we'd better leave."

"If that's what you want," he murmured.

"Did you think I asked you over here to—" She stopped abruptly.

"To make love to you?" He completed her sentence.

"Well . . . yes."

"I didn't think I could be that fortunate." He looked at her curiously. "Why *did* you ask me, Meredith? I can't believe you couldn't find anyone else to play in the woods with you."

"I didn't try," she admitted.

He grinned. "Then if you don't want my body, what *do* you want? Until now, I've had to force my company on you."

"I know. I suddenly realized I've been a royal pain in the ankle," she answered honestly.

"I wouldn't say that."

"Because you're too polite."

"No, because I enjoy being with you," he answered quietly.

"I enjoy your company, too, Jeremy. That's why I decided to stop acting like a spoiled brat. I'd like to be friends instead of adversaries."

A little smile lifted the corners of his firm mouth. "I'd like to be a great deal more than that, but I'll settle for whatever you're willing to give me."

She held out her hand. "Let's agree on friendship for now."

"For now," he repeated, enveloping her small hand in his large one.

Meredith wasn't ready to let down her defenses completely. The potent attraction between them couldn't be denied, but there had to be more than that. She withdrew her hand quickly. Even that small contact was inflammatory.

"Shall we go?" she asked.

"I think we'd better before I carry you kicking and scratching into the bedroom."

"I'm not worried. You're much too civilized for that."

"Don't count on it. You never know what dark currents run rampant under a civilized man's facade."

His remark wasn't meant to be taken seriously—or was it? Meredith was suddenly shaken by the flash of implacability that hardened his features. The expression was so fleeting that she might have imagined it. Mischief was in his eyes now, not menace.

"As long as you're not interested in making mad, passionate love, we might as well get started," he remarked.

The road to Muir Woods wound through peaceful countryside dotted with small towns. Jeremy drove competently, but swiftly, until Meredith complained.

"We aren't in any hurry," she pointed out. "The idea isn't to set a new speed record."

"How can you fly a plane, and be nervous in a car?" he asked, but he slowed down.

"I consider flying safer, but I'm not nervous. I simply want to enjoy the countryside. I love being outdoors on a day like this."

Although the air was crisp, bright sunshine cast a golden glow over the landscape. It was a perfect northern California day, cool, clear and picturesquely beautiful.

Jeremy turned his head to glance at her. "You look right at home in the country."

"So do you." She smiled slightly. "That proves you can't judge a man by his jogging suit."

"Why would you say that?"

"Because you're only here today to please me."

"I can't deny that, but why would you think I'd rather be someplace else?"

"This isn't your kind of thing. You live life in the fast lane."

"I don't know why everyone gets that impression of me." His voice held mild irritation.

"Perhaps because you're like your car—high-powered and glitzy."

She studied him clinically. Jeremy was like some magnificent animal at rest. His long body was relaxed in the leather bucket seat, but there was still an alertness about him, as though he would spring into action at the first hint of prey.

"That makes me sound very superficial," he protested.

"Far from it. You're the most complicated man I've ever met," she said frankly. "I wonder if I'll ever get to know you."

"I thought we'd found out quite a lot about each other. I know you're quick-tempered, yet loyal. That you hate taking orders, but you're extremely good in a crisis. Oh, and one more thing. You never learned to cook," he teased.

"And what do I know about you?" she asked quietly.

"If it's trivia you want, I'll be happy to supply it. Let's see . . . you already know I sleep in the nude."

Meredith realized he wasn't going to reveal anything meaningful about himself. She suppressed a sigh. "Never mind. Tell me about your trip to Phoenix instead. I've never been there."

"You'd like it, it's a lovely city."

"What did you do for your parents' anniversary?"

"They had a party at home." His eyes narrowed slightly as he stared at the road. "Reach into the glove compartment and get out the road map, will you? I want to be sure we're going the right way."

She did as he said, although he hadn't shown any indecision until then. Was it a ploy to change the subject? But why? He'd talked freely about his parents before. Meredith was suddenly impatient with herself. Hadn't she vowed to stop hunting for paper dragons?

They reached Muir Woods a short time later and found the lovely wilderness area almost deserted. It was often crowded in summer, but not many people were drawn there on a Monday afternoon in winter. The towering redwood trees diffused the sun, filtering the light on the sylvan paths that were carpeted with moss and pine needles.

"Aren't these redwoods awesome?" Meredith asked as they strolled along one of the trails that cut through the forest. "It's hard to believe some of these trees are a thousand years old. Do you realize they've been standing here since the year nine hundred?"

"They survived forest fires, floods and tornadoes," Jeremy agreed. "The miracle is that they survived modern man and his bulldozers."

"Thank goodness for conservationists like John Muir. It seems incomprehensible that people wanted to chop down these magnificent giants to rebuild San Francisco after the 1906 earthquake and fire."

"Luckily we've learned to appreciate our national treasures more." He squinted up at the leafy canopy far away.

Meredith followed his lead, tilting her head back until she almost lost her balance.

Jeremy's arms closed around her as she lurched backward. "Careful," he admonished. "You're going to land right on your pretty backside."

"I was trying to see the tops of the trees."

He guided her head to his shoulder and supported her chin in his hand. "Is that better?" he asked, smiling down at her.

His head was poised directly over hers. "Yes, I...they're magnificent, aren't they?"

"A triumph of nature," he murmured, brushing her forehead with his lips.

Meredith's legs felt suddenly boneless. She shivered as weakness spread through the rest of her body.

His expression changed to concern. "You're cold."

He turned her in his arms. After unzipping his windbreaker, he drew her against his body and wrapped the jacket around her. Instant heat flashed through Meredith but it wasn't transferred from Jeremy, it was generated by him. She was aware of every hard masculine angle making an impression even through her heavy clothing. The contact became still more inflaming when he rubbed her back briskly. The sensitive tips of her breasts were crushed repeatedly against the solid wall of his chest.

"Maybe we'd better turn back," he said. "It's pretty nippy today."

She drew away without looking at him. "I'm all right now. I just had a chill for a minute."

"I don't want you to catch cold."

"I won't," she promised. "Let's go see if we can spot a salmon."

The small sign beside Redwood Creek proclaimed it one of the few remaining salmon streams in the San Francisco Bay area. Fresh, clear water tumbled over submerged rocks, and the air was perfumed with the pungent scent of laurel and pine. They sat down on a fallen log, searching for orange flashes in the sparkling stream.

After a short time Meredith pointed and exclaimed, "There's one!"

"Big bruiser, isn't he?" Jeremy commented admiringly.

"I wonder why it's so exciting to see something in its wild state." She continued to stare intently into the water.

"It's man's primitive instinct to hunt."

"But I'm a woman, and I feel the thrill."

"Women are as predatory as men."

"I don't believe that." She turned then to look at him.

"History has recorded some mighty cold-blooded women, going all the way back to Delilah. And how about Ma Barker and Lizzie Borden, to name just a couple of modern miscreants."

"I suppose you're right, but they were exceptions. The average person couldn't commit a crime, regardless of gender."

"There is no such thing as an average person. It also depends on what you call a crime. Jaywalking is against the law. So are certain forms of sex."

She colored slightly. "You know that's not what we're talking about."

"I was simply pointing out that your 'average person' isn't always law-abiding."

"Maybe not, but he couldn't do something truly evil. Could you commit murder?" she demanded.

Jeremy didn't answer immediately. When he did, his answer chilled Meredith. "No one really knows what he's capable of under certain circumstances."

"What circumstances could possibly justify murder?"

"Different ones for you than for me—just as we'd carry out the crime differently. Men are more apt to use force than women."

She felt a ripple of fear as a change seemed to come over him. His cold, hard eyes and sharpened cheekbones turned him into a stranger—a dangerous one. Her recoil was an automatic reflex.

She jumped to her feet. "It's getting late. We'd better go."

Jeremy stood up, too, towering over her with a smile she didn't find reassuring. "Why the sudden hurry? We've only hunted down one salmon."

"I don't care. I just want to get out of here."

She backed away from him, inadvertently stumbling over the fallen log. When his hands reached out to steady her, Meredith panicked.

"Leave me alone!" she ordered in a high, thin voice.

He dropped his arms, staring at her in amazement. "What's wrong, Meredith?"

The unreasoning fear fled as she gazed into his concerned face. This was Jeremy, the man she'd learned to depend on in a crisis, not some maniac murderer. How could she have let her imagination run away with her like that?

"Nothing's wrong," she mumbled. "I . . . I got cold again."

"That's not the reason." He gazed searchingly at her. "Something upset you. What was it?"

She laughed slightly. "I guess all that talk about upstanding citizens turning into criminals made me wonder what I was capable of."

"No, it made you wonder what *I* was." A muscle jerked in his tight jaw. "Do you really think I'd hurt you, Meredith?"

"Not really, but for a moment you looked so ruthless," she said uncertainly. "I know it's crazy, but I could almost imagine you . . . well, doing something violent."

A slight frown creased his forehead. "It never occurred to me that you'd be afraid of me. I'm extremely sorry."

"You needn't be. It was all in my mind," she said earnestly. "You didn't do anything."

"But you thought I was going to, that's the point. I'm rather stunned."

"You're making too much of this, Jeremy," she pleaded. "It was simply a misunderstanding. Can't we forget the whole thing?"

He stared at her consideringly. "I suppose that depends on whether *you* can."

She could tell his feelings were hurt, which was understandable. She'd acted as though he were an ax murderer or something.

"I've apologized," she said penitently. "What more can I do?"

His stern features relaxed as he gazed into her beautiful, pleading face. "That's a rash question. How do you know what I'll answer?"

"I trust you, Jeremy," she answered simply.

He folded her in his arms and buried his face in her hair, groaning. "You're so sweet, little Meredith, and all I've done is take advantage of you. If you had any sense you'd tell me to get lost."

When she could extricate herself enough from his smothering embrace to lift her head, she smiled up at him. "My life wouldn't be nearly as interesting without you."

"You've given new meaning to mine, that's for sure," he replied in a husky voice.

As his lips touched hers, Meredith's heart swelled with happiness. It was a tender kiss that meant more than the passionate ones that had aroused her. In some dimly sensed way, she knew they'd made a breakthrough in their relationship. Jeremy finally felt something for her besides desire.

His lips clung to hers for a long moment before he lifted his head. "You're very special to me," he said quietly, confirming her conviction.

She gave a breathy little laugh to cover how moved she was. "It's nice to know I'm more than a convenience."

"If I told you how much more, you might be scared for a different reason."

Jeremy put his arm around her shoulders as they re-traced their steps in a companionable silence. No more words were needed.

The sun was setting when they returned to the car. "What would you like to do now?" he asked.

"I didn't have anything else in mind," she answered.

"How about an early movie, and dinner afterward?"

"That sounds perfect."

Instead of going back to the city, Jeremy stopped in a little town along the way. A movie theater was showing a comedy neither of them had seen. The excellent reviews it had received were merited. They ate popcorn and laughed uproariously.

"That was an inspired choice," Meredith remarked when they came out of the theater.

"I hope we'll be as lucky with a restaurant. Keep an eye out for something that looks good."

They finally settled on a small Italian bistro set back from the highway. It didn't look particularly prepossessing, but it was either that or one of the fast-food places that had sprung up every few miles like neon mushrooms.

The interior was a pleasant surprise. It was softly lit by shaded lamps on round tables, and a delicious aroma of garlic and spices drifted tantalizingly from the kitchen.

A smiling Italian man led them to a table covered with a red-and-white checked cloth. He presented them with menus, then left to go into the kitchen. A few moments later he returned with a basket of warm bread and a crock of sweet butter.

"Mmm, this is divine," Meredith said after sampling the crusty bread. "If the rest of the food is as good, I'll have one of everything—except the calamari."

"Don't you like squid? It's an Italian favorite."

"Not with me. It tastes like old rubber bands, and it looks awful in the supermarket." She wrinkled her nose. "All those legs with suckers on them. I walk by with my eyes closed."

"When was the last time you were in a supermarket?" Jeremy teased.

"I drop in now and then to pick up men," she answered mischievously. "The frozen food department is a great place to meet bachelors."

"You're not supposed to be looking for one."

"Maybe not right now, but a girl has to look to the future," she answered lightly.

"You don't expect our romance to last?" He matched her casual tone.

"It will be a shock to my friends when it's over," she replied, evading the question. "They think you're wonderful. It won't be easy to explain what went wrong."

"Perhaps nothing will," he said smoothly.

"I don't think I'd like being engaged for the rest of my life."

As Jeremy hesitated, the waiter reappeared, saving him the necessity of a reply.

"Are you ready to order?" the man asked pleasantly. "The catch of the day is petrale sole. We also have fresh salmon." He went on to recite a number of house specialties.

"I think I'll have the pasta with prawns and mushrooms," Meredith said.

"That sounds good to me, too," Jeremy agreed.

Then they decided on hearts of palm rather than the house salad. Jeremy made a selection from the wine list. After the waiter left to fill their orders, they didn't return to the subject they'd been discussing.

"When am I going to see you again?" Jeremy asked.

"Didn't you reach your saturation point today?"

He smiled. "Stop fishing for compliments."

"Can't you think of any?" she pouted.

"None that I care to mention here."

"You could tell me something flowery—like my eyes are the color of emeralds," she joked.

"They are, and your anatomy is equally spectacular." He transferred his gaze to her sweater. "You have the most beautiful breasts I've ever seen—or would like to see, I should say."

Meredith felt her cheeks turn pink. "That wasn't the kind of compliment I was fishing for."

"I was only being honest."

"Can't you be honest without being so frank?" she asked plaintively.

"I don't know why that should embarrass you. You don't have a single visible flaw. I imagine you're perfection in the nude."

She gave an awkward laugh. "How am I supposed to answer that?"

"You could let me judge for myself," he said softly.

"We've strayed pretty far off the subject," she remarked reprovingly.

His eyes danced with devilry. "I must confess I've forgotten what it was."

"You were asking when we were going to see each other again."

"When are we?"

"Thursday night if you're free. There's a charity affair at the Fairmont Hotel, a dinner dance to benefit the Foundation for the Arts. Evelyn is on the fund-raising committee. She phoned over the weekend to find out if we could come, but I told her I'd have to ask you first."

"It's fine with me," he answered.

Meredith was reminded of what she wanted to ask him. "I would have called you, but I don't have your private number. Is there any reason you're not listed in the telephone book?"

He shrugged. "Everyone I want to hear from has my number."

"I don't."

"I'll give it to you." He smiled. "You're the one I want to hear from most."

She looked at him curiously. "You're a very private person, aren't you?"

"I suppose you could say that." The waiter arrived with their salads, and Jeremy regarded his approvingly. "Looks great, doesn't it?"

Meredith was filled with a familiar feeling of frustration. Every time she was about to get a clue to the real Jeremy under the smooth exterior, something happened to thwart her. Was it simply bad timing on every occasion? Or was he adept at turning situations to his advantage? She sighed and picked up her salad fork.

They dined leisurely and lingered over coffee and dessert, but it was still only nine-thirty when they drove up to Meredith's apartment.

"Would you like to come in?" she asked as they walked up the path to her front door.

"I'd like to, but I'd better go home and check my phone messages." He took her key and opened the door. "In case there were any crises while I was gone."

"I hope not. I'd feel responsible."

"Today was worth a full-blown catastrophe."

As his head inclined toward hers, the phone started to ring. She turned toward it automatically, then stopped and gazed up at him. "I had a wonderful time, Jeremy."

"Aren't you going to answer the phone?"

"The machine will pick it up."

"Go ahead and answer it, I can wait." He followed her inside and closed the door.

The caller was Paula. After finding out she only wanted to chat, Meredith promised to call her back.

"I should have gone home and let you talk," Jeremy said when she returned.

"She didn't have anything special on her mind, and I wanted to say goodbye properly."

He moved toward her with a slow smile. "It sounds as though you have something special planned."

"No, I only. . . I mean, you took the whole day off for me. The least I can do is say thank-you." She suddenly felt like a tongue-tied teenager on her first date. Was it that apparent that she didn't want him to leave?

He put his hands on her shoulders. "You don't have to thank me for anything. I'm the one who is in *your* debt."

"Is that why you came today?" she asked in a small voice.

"You must know better than that. I was flattered that you wanted to be with me."

"We did have fun, didn't we?"

He drew her slightly closer. "We always do."

"Not always, but we will from now on."

"That sounds very promising," he murmured.

"You know what I mean," she protested.

"I know what I'd like you to mean." Tiny lights flickered in his eyes as he gazed down at her.

"I was trying to assure you there won't be any more unpleasantness like there was at Evelyn's party."

He grinned. "When you called me a sex-starved alley cat?"

Had she really said that? Jeremy would never have trouble obtaining sex. She smiled wryly. "I tend to get a little graphic when I'm annoyed."

"Will you be angry all over again if I say I was gratified?"

"I'm sure it's very satisfying to have women chasing you."

"The part I enjoyed was that you seemed to care." His hands on her shoulders became caressing.

"I suppose women are territorial as well as predatory. You're teaching me a lot about myself."

"I could teach you things you never guessed about yourself." His warm breath fanned her mouth.

She moistened her lips unconsciously. "I'm not sure I like the things I'm finding out."

"That you're a warm, responsive woman? I've never found anyone so enchantingly receptive." His arms circled her waist, drawing her against him.

Meredith's hands splayed out over his chest in an automatic defense mechanism, putting a sliver of distance between their bodies. "That's merely a tribute to your expertise."

"I couldn't create what wasn't already there."

Her heart was beating at an alarming rate. "I'm usually fairly inhibited," she insisted, although it wasn't true. She'd simply never met anyone who affected her as Jeremy did.

"Shall I show you how wrong you are?"

His mouth closed over hers, proving his point. After the briefest instant of resistance, Meredith's lips parted. Instead of holding him off, her hands moved over his chest in a sensuous exploration. Everything had been building up to this moment. How could she deny what she wanted so badly?

Her response brought a low sound of satisfaction from Jeremy. His kiss grew more intimate, more demanding. His tongue probed then withdrew, tantalizing her with a promise that made her senses reel. She followed his tongue with her own in an erotic game that threatened to spiral out of control. When he finally dragged his mouth away and buried his face in her neck, she clung to him trembling.

"Sweet, sweet Meredith," he breathed. "You're utterly bewitching."

"You're the magician. I act differently with you," she said helplessly.

His golden eyes held hers hypnotically. "What we have is very special. You know that, don't you?"

Special was a pallid word to describe it. Every fiber cried out for his touch? She tried to maintain some grip on reality, but when his mouth possessed hers once more, only Jeremy seemed important.

She was lost in a world of sensation that heightened as his hand cupped her breast. The slow, knowledgeable movement of his fingers brought spasms of pleasure that intensified when he bent his head to nuzzle the diamond-hard peak with his lips. The barrier of her sweater made the feeling even more stimulating somehow.

After an inflaming few moments he pushed her sweater up and pulled her blouse out of her jeans. As his hand slid underneath to caress her bare skin, Meredith caught her breath. She had never felt so completely wanton before. The urge to tear his shirt open was truly shocking. She could hardly wait to feel their bodies merge, with no impediment to blunt the inexpressible feeling.

Some vestige of self-preservation restrained her. Jeremy mustn't know how completely he could subjugate her. As he started to unbutton her blouse, she stiffened with the effort at self-control.

His response was unexpected. When her body became rigid, he paused. Then he pulled her sweater down and held her in a loose embrace. "Forgive me, angel. You're enough to make any man lose his head."

"I . . . it's all right," she mumbled.

"I should have said good-night on the doorstep." He kissed her cheek before releasing her. "I'll see you Thursday night."

"You're leaving?" She couldn't comprehend what was happening.

"Don't you think I'd better?" He laughed ruefully. "That's a rhetorical question if ever I heard one. We both know the answer."

Meredith stared at the door after he left, unable to comprehend what had happened. Jeremy wanted her— she couldn't be wrong about that. Then *why*? She was always asking herself that. The answer was the same; he obviously didn't want to get involved. Fortunately for her, he had a conscience, since a man that experienced would realize she couldn't refuse him. Meredith knew she should be grateful, but it was one of Jeremy's nobler instincts she found difficult to appreciate at that moment.

He didn't look any more pleased with himself. After getting into his car he stared at the quiet street, frowning. After a short time he reached for the door handle, then hesitated. A long moment later he started the engine and drove away.

Chapter Seven

Meredith was in a foul mood the next day. Clara watched without comment as she slammed around the office with a face like a storm cloud.

Finally the older woman said, "A day off didn't do you a lot of good. You're as tense as a virgin on her wedding night. What's wrong, Meredith?"

"Nothing, I'm just bored." She jumped up and went over to stare out the window. "My first charter isn't for another two hours."

"You didn't have to come in this early," Clara pointed out.

Meredith shrugged. "I didn't have anything to do at home."

"I wish I could say the same. My ironing is piled up to the ceiling. I don't suppose you iron or do windows?" Clara tried to jolly her out of whatever was bothering her.

Meredith wasn't really listening. "I send everything to the laundry."

Clara sighed. "I hope your group is early."

"I'll settle for them being on time for a change."

"If you don't stop looking so gloomy they're all going to ask for parachutes, and we don't have enough to go around."

Meredith smiled reluctantly. "I'll tell them a parachute wouldn't do them any good over water."

"That ought to be good for repeat business."

"What there is of it," Meredith remarked dejectedly.

Clara slanted a shuttered glance at her. "I assume you were out with Jeremy yesterday. Is he responsible for your present lack of goodwill toward men?"

"Yes I was, and no he isn't. I mean, there's nothing wrong with me," Meredith insisted.

The telephone rang, putting an end to the discussion, Meredith hoped. Clara answered it, then handed the phone to her without comment.

Jeremy's cheery voice greeted her. He, at least, wasn't suffering from any doubts. "Good morning, angel. How are you doing this morning? No bad effects from yesterday?"

Her slim body tensed. "What do you mean?"

"I hope you didn't catch cold."

"Oh . . . no, I'm fine."

"You're better than that." His voice deepened. "You're great!"

She wasn't about to be flimflammed again. Whatever game Jeremy was playing was wearing thin. "I'm rather busy right now," she said coolly. "Did you want something special?"

"Just to tell you how much I enjoyed yesterday."

"I hope I didn't keep you out too late," she answered ironically.

"I wish I could have stayed." His voice held regret.

Meredith was outraged. There had been nothing stopping him, as he very well knew! She could keep up the fiction if he could, however. "We had such a full day. All I wanted to do was take a shower and go to bed. I'll bet I was asleep before you even got home."

"You were more fortunate than I." His voice held rueful amusement. "I was awake half the night thinking about you. When am I going to see you again?"

"We have a date on Thursday." She kept her voice level with an effort.

"That's too far away. I have an appointment this evening, but how about tomorrow night?"

Anger threatened her self-control. Jeremy pretended to be eager for her company, but other people always took precedence. "*I'm* busy tomorrow night," she replied stiffly.

"Thursday seems such a long way off," he complained. "But if that's the best you can do."

Meredith was even more depressed after she hung up. Thursday *was* a long way off. Had she acted childishly? Her refusal to meet before then had obviously cost her more than it had him. Jeremy's protest had been a token one. Then what was the point in rubbing salt in the wound if their relationship wasn't going anywhere?

Meredith spent a miserable couple of days, but as Thursday approached her spirits lifted. By the time Jeremy came to pick her up that night she was tingling with anticipation.

The dress she'd chosen was guaranteed to catch any man's attention. The puckered, white lace top molded her torso like a second skin, emphasizing her firm breasts and slim midriff. The bouffant, triple-tiered skirt of emerald taffeta was more demure, except that it barely grazed her knees, revealing long lengths of leg.

Jeremy's reaction was everything she could have wished. He barely restrained himself from whistling as his avid gaze went over her from shining curls to spike-heeled sandals.

"You do fantastic things for that dress," he said finally.

"This old thing?" She laughed mischievously. "It's just something I found hanging in my closet."

"I like your taste in old clothes." He chuckled.

Meredith knew, without conceit, that they made a handsome couple. Jeremy's impressive physique and interesting face would garner as many admiring glances from women as she received from men.

She saw it happen when they joined her friends at a large table in the grand ballroom. But the men greeted him warmly, too, accepting him as a member of the group. Jeremy had charmed everyone completely.

She referred to the fact while they were dancing. "You're very talented with people."

He raised one dark eyebrow. "I'm not sure what that means."

"Everyone likes you."

He smiled. "Including you, I hope."

"Let's just say I don't find it a hardship being with you," she answered lightly.

"Is that the best you can do?"

"I don't want you to get conceited."

"How can I help it when I'm with the most beautiful woman here?" he murmured, drawing her closer.

"That's shameless flattery, but I wouldn't mind hearing more."

Meredith felt like purring as her body conformed to Jeremy's. All the irritation and uncertainty of the past few days was washed away by the joy of being near him.

"Shall I tell you how much I've been looking forward to tonight?" His long fingers stroked the sensitive skin behind her ear. "I missed you this week."

"What did you do?" She tried to pretend his sensuous caress wasn't affecting her.

"Thought about you when I should have been working. Did you think about me?"

"Once or twice," she admitted.

"I was available." His lips brushed her forehead. "I gave you my number."

"I only wanted it for emergencies," she protested faintly. The slow movement of his body against hers was raising her pulse rate.

"I think we're safely past those."

"The black sedan still follows me wherever I go."

"It won't for much longer," he soothed.

A little chill contracted her heart. "Is your deal nearing completion?"

"I hope so."

"How long do we . . . I mean, when do you think it will be?"

"A couple of weeks should do it."

"I see." Meredith had the bleak sense of time slipping away. Would she ever see Jeremy again when this was all over?

He tipped her chin up. "You said being with me wasn't a hardship."

"It isn't," she murmured.

"Then why are you looking so tragic?"

"That's hunger you're seeing. These big charity events test your staying power. Do you think they'll ever serve dinner?" She smiled to mask her true feelings.

He chuckled. "You're in a hurry for rubber chicken and overcooked peas?"

"Maybe we'll be lucky and they'll serve overcooked roast beef and rubber carrots."

"I'll buy you a hamburger after we leave," he promised, leading her off the dance floor with an arm around her shoulders.

The evening was so perfect that Meredith hated to see it end. She and Jeremy were the last people at their large table except for Evelyn and Don.

"We're stuck here till the bitter end, but you don't have to stay," Evelyn advised them.

"Never marry a woman who lets herself get railroaded onto committees." Don smothered a yawn. "Go on home, you lucky dogs."

"I suppose we should." Meredith repressed a sigh. "Tomorrow's a working day."

Jeremy could see her reluctance. "Why don't we have one more dance?"

They circled the floor slowly, completely absorbed in each other. Neither spoke because no words were necessary. They were content simply to be together.

When they were in the car going home he reached out for her hand, as though wanting to remain in contact. "That was the best charity affair I ever attended."

"In spite of the rubber chicken?" she teased. "You were right about the menu."

"No one expects the food at these things to be edible. I promised you a hamburger, didn't I?"

"I'm not hungry. Are you?"

"Not really, but I wouldn't mind a cup of coffee."

"You'd better take me home," she answered regretfully. It would be very late by the time Jeremy drove to the suburbs and back. "It's too bad you don't live in Marin," she said. "It must be a drag for you, having to make two round-trips."

He turned his head and gave her a melting smile. "I'd do a lot more for a night like this. Besides, I get to spend more time with you."

"Have you ever considered moving next door?" she asked lightly, although her heart soared at the evidence that Jeremy didn't want the evening to end either.

"I thought perhaps—" He broke off abruptly as the cars ahead of them slowed to a crawl. "Uh-oh, I don't like the looks of this. Traffic should be light at this time of night." He flicked on the radio and tuned it to a news station.

Meredith groaned. "I hope nothing happened on Doyle Drive. That always causes a mess."

As they inched forward, the newscast finished with the national news and turned to local events. After reporting a warehouse fire and a minor disturbance at a rock concert, the newscaster said: "Here's a traffic update on that accident on the Golden Gate Bridge. All lanes are closed in both directions, causing a massive backup. Motorists are advised to take alternate routes. Two people have been reported injured, and an ambulance is trying to get to the scene. The California Highway Patrol estimates it will be at least an hour before traffic is flowing freely again."

"Now what do we do?" Meredith exclaimed.

"First of all, we get off this street." Jeremy made a right turn as soon as they crept up to the corner. "It looks as though we're going to have that coffee whether we want it or not."

"We could be sitting around for hours," she fretted. "Their estimates are always wrong."

"The only other route is over the Bay Bridge, through Oakland and over the Richmond Bridge to Marin."

"That's as bad as waiting for them to clear the road. It would take forever."

"I have one other suggestion. You can stay at my house tonight." As she turned to look at him sharply he said, "Doesn't that make more sense than driving around all night?"

"I suppose so," she agreed slowly.

"Feel free to cheer loudly," he remarked in a dry voice.

"It isn't the ideal solution," she protested.

"Your reputation won't be tarnished. We're engaged, remember?"

"I'm not worried about my reputation," she muttered.

The thought of sleeping under the same roof with Jeremy was upsetting. She'd had lurid enough fantasies alone in her own apartment! Tension replaced the warm relaxed feeling she'd had all night.

He glanced at her with a raised eyebrow. "My suggestion wasn't made out of any ulterior motive. I don't expect you to share my bed."

"I know that," she replied distantly.

"Then what's the problem?"

The intimate circumstances obviously didn't bother *him*. Meredith searched for a valid reason for her perturbation, and finally found one. "How will I get home in the morning?"

"I'll take you," he said, disposing of her last objection.

Walking up to the front door next to Jeremy was a poignant experience for Meredith. They could almost have been a comfortably married couple coming home after a pleasant evening out. Except for the knots in her stomach. Married people went upstairs to bed—together.

If Jeremy's thoughts ran along those lines he masked them admirably. Turning to her in the foyer he said, "Do you want to reconsider about that cup of coffee?"

"You mean you want me to make it?" She laughed nervously. "You don't know how to use the coffee maker, and you hate instant."

"You remembered," he said softly.

"How could I forget? It's the first thing I found out about you the night I came here. That's not so long ago."

"I can't believe we've known each other such a short time," he marveled.

"It was a whirlwind courtship all right," she answered wryly.

Something flickered in his amber eyes. "That's what I had in mind. I'm a very determined man."

"I found that out." She turned toward the staircase. "If you'll point me toward the nearest guest room, I'd like to go to sleep."

The familiar sexual tension was beginning to crackle between them, but Meredith didn't want to fall into Jeremy's bed merely because circumstances made it convenient. If they made love it should be a spontaneous happening, a passion they couldn't deny. He could rouse that feeling in her easily enough, but it had to be mutual—and from what she could see, it wasn't.

He followed her up the stairs without protest, and indicated a bedroom down the hall from his. The room was charmingly decorated with French provincial furniture that added to the feminine feeling. The double bed had a pink-and-rose-flowered spread, and white organdy curtains covered the windows.

"This is lovely," Meredith observed.

"It was my sister Charlotte's room." He opened a door to an adjoining bathroom tiled in matching pink. "There are more towels in the cabinet under the sink, and a new toothbrush in the medicine chest."

"That's a blessing," she said appreciatively.

He opened a mirrored cabinet on the wall. "You might also find some of this stuff useful."

A brief glimpse revealed bubble bath, hair spray and shampoo. Jeremy provided his female guests with any items they forgot to bring along, Meredith thought dryly.

"Do you need anything else?" he asked.

"I don't suppose you have a spare nightgown?" Her cynical tone indicated she already knew the answer. That was one item he didn't expect to be required.

He grinned. "Sorry, I never use them. Would a pajama top do?"

"I thought you didn't wear pajamas."

"Everyone has to have one pair in case of illness. You're in luck. Since I'm remarkably healthy, mine is brand-new. Come with me."

She followed him down the hall to his room where he rummaged in a bureau drawer and brought out a pair of white silk pajamas.

Holding the top up to her, he tipped his head consideringly. "It won't be the greatest fit in the world."

"That's all right, I'll roll up the sleeves. Thanks for the loan."

"My pleasure." He smiled. "Anything else I can do for you?"

The question wasn't meant to be suggestive. Or was it? "No, I . . . uh . . . good night." She left the room abruptly, furious at herself for losing her cool, and at Jeremy for being amused by the fact.

In her own room, Meredith undressed and hung her gown in the closet, groaning. She only hoped none of her neighbors were around when she arrived home in the morning after obviously spending the night with someone. It was a vain hope, for they'd be just leaving for work at that hour.

As she stripped off her panty hose and reached for the white silk top, Meredith paused. Did bankers go to work late? She hadn't asked Jeremy what time he was taking her home. In any case, she'd better have an alarm clock. Assuming she managed to fall asleep, it would take something drastic to wake her after this traumatic night!

A thorough search of the bedroom turned up every amenity except an alarm clock. She'd have to ask Jeremy for one. The last thing Meredith wanted was another encounter with him, but there didn't seem to be any other choice. It would be a lot worse to have him come in and wake her in the morning before her defenses were in place.

She stood in the middle of the floor indecisively. It seemed like a lot of bother to get dressed again. After all, she was adequately covered. His top reached almost to her knees. The only problem was, the first button didn't start till below her breastbone, leaving a decidedly plunging neckline. It wasn't actually revealing, though, and if she didn't hurry, Jeremy would be asleep. That was the deciding factor.

A line of light under his door reassured her, and she knocked lightly.

"Come in," he called.

Jeremy was lying in bed reading. The covers were pulled up only to his waist, leaving his chest and shoulders bare. The bedside lamp cast a pool of light over his torso, while the rest of the room was in intimate darkness. Meredith paused in the doorway, her mouth dry.

"Excuse me for not getting up." His smile held gentle mockery. "Do you need something?"

"I'd like to borrow an alarm clock."

"I'll wake you," he offered.

"No, I . . . I might want to get up before you do."

He frowned slightly. "I don't have another clock, but you can take mine." He indicated an electric clock on the bedside next to him.

"Then how will you get up?"

"You can wake *me*."

While she was considering the pros and cons of the idea, he turned on his side and reached for the plug behind the nightstand. The covers pulled away, revealing the long line of his back and one hip. Jeremy hadn't been lying about sleeping in the nude.

"I can do that," she said hastily as he seemed in danger of toppling out of bed.

The plug was near the baseboard and resisted her nervously fumbling fingers. When she finally pulled it loose and started to straighten up, Meredith realized that the whole front of her pajama top was gaping open. Jeremy's fascinated gaze was riveted on her bare body, which was visible almost to her thighs.

She stood erect, clutching her lapels together, her cheeks flaming. "I might have known you'd pull a cheap trick like this," she stormed illogically.

"I was trying to disconnect the clock for you," he said helplessly.

"You were staring at me like a Peeping Tom!"

"I wouldn't have been human if I hadn't." He smiled.

"You might have the decency to apologize," she exclaimed in outrage.

"What man could help himself? You have the body of a goddess."

"Don't try to get around me. You've been making suggestive remarks ever since we got here. I'm beginning to think your invitation to spend the night wasn't so innocent after all."

"Have I made the slightest pass at you?" he asked quietly.

She had to admit he hadn't, but Meredith was in no mood to be rational. Her own behavior embarrassed her, not his, which was even more humiliating.

"It's just as bad not knowing if you're going to pounce on me in the middle of the night," she muttered, recognizing the absurdity of her statement.

Jeremy did, too. "You don't really believe that."

"I'm going to bed," she said abruptly, wanting only to end the conversation.

"Meredith, wait!" When she kept on going, he leaped out of bed and caught her arm. "This whole thing was simply an amusing incident. You must know you can trust me."

Jeremy was completely unself-conscious about his nude state, but Meredith couldn't match his aplomb. She kept her eyes fixed on his face so they wouldn't be tempted to stray to his splendid body, only inches from hers. A brief glimpse had made her quiveringly aware of every well-proportioned segment.

His hands grasped her shoulders. "We were so close tonight. I felt we'd finally reached an understanding. Don't let something like this spoil it," he coaxed.

"I guess I overreacted because I was embarrassed," she conceded, getting the words out with difficulty.

"You have no reason to be." He framed her face in his palms and gazed at her tenderly. "You're absolute perfection."

How could he be so relaxed when every nerve in her body was jangling? She swallowed painfully. "You'd better get back in bed before you catch cold."

"Don't worry, angel. I won't try to make love to you. I hope someday you'll change your mind, but you made your feelings clear the last time I tried."

Meredith's eyes widened. "What do you mean?"

"I felt the way you panicked when I touched you."

"Was *that* why you left?"

He smiled wryly. "My willpower isn't limitless."

"You would have made love to me if you'd thought I was willing?"

His expression altered as he gazed at her mouth. "You can't have any doubt about that."

"Oh, Jeremy." She laughed helplessly. "I thought you were knowledgeable about women."

His hands gripped her shoulders again, urgently this time. "I have to be sure I know what you're saying."

"I didn't want you to go that night," she answered softly. "I thought you left because you didn't want to get any more involved with me."

He drew her into his arms and buried his face in her hair, groaning. "How much more involved can I be? I think I've fallen in love with you."

She stared at him, almost in shock. Everything was happening too fast. His assault on her physical senses must have slowed down her brain process. "You...you love me?" she faltered.

He raised his head to look deeply into her eyes. "Since the night we flew through the storm together, although I didn't realize it at the time."

"You didn't call me afterward," she said doubtfully. "*I* was the one who came looking for *you*."

"You know why I stayed away. I didn't want you mixed up in this dirty business."

It crossed her mind that it was a strange way to refer to a business deal, but she couldn't think with his hardened body distracting her. "Please get back in bed, Jeremy—or at least put on a robe."

His lips brushed hers in a tantalizing caress that stopped short of being a kiss. "Is that what you really want?"

"I . . . I don't know," she admitted breathlessly.

He kissed her then, parting her lips for a slow exploration that blotted out all objections. They seemed pointless anyway when his hands moved over her back, tracing its slender length to the gentle swell of her buttocks. This was the reality of all her fantasies.

"We belong together, sweetheart." His warm mouth slid over her cheek. "You must know that by now."

When he lifted the hem of the pajama top and gently stroked her bottom, she arched her body into his. The sharp thrust increased his already evident desire. With a swift movement he pushed her top up until it bunched under her arms. The thin barrier that had separated them was removed.

Meredith started to tremble as a hot tide of almost primitive passion enveloped her. The sensation of her bare breasts against his chest was exquisitely arousing. She wanted to experience more of him, to caress every part of him. Her hands followed his lead, exploring, savoring, stroking sensuously.

He drew in his breath sharply. "Sweet Meredith, you're driving me wild."

"Show me how wild," she whispered.

He crushed her so close there was no doubt. "You want me, too," he exulted.

"For so long." She sighed. "Don't leave me again."

"Never again," he promised, drawing away, but only to unbutton the pajama top.

Pushing it off her shoulders he stared at her with eyes so molten that her legs felt boneless. She held out her arms, but Jeremy didn't pull her close. His avid gaze devoured her as he feathered her body with his fingertips, tracing the length of her neck, the slope of her shoulders, the tender hollow in her throat.

When his hands moved down to her breasts she made a breathy sound. And when he bent his head to touch his tongue to one coral tip, she moaned softly and tangled her fingers in his hair.

"That feels so..." She couldn't express herself.

"I know, darling."

He knelt in front of her, gripping her hips while his mouth continued its slow devastation. Meredith was grateful for his support, because she couldn't have maintained her balance when he trailed a burning string of kisses over her stomach. After dipping his tongue into her navel, he moved lower. His hands traced the length of her thighs while his mouth found her most vulnerable part.

"Please, Jeremy," she gasped. "I can't take much more."

"You're like a dream come true." He stood up and lifted her into his arms. "Do you know how it makes me feel to see you respond like this?"

"I've never wanted anyone so much." She clasped her arms around his neck.

"Nor I, my love."

He got into bed still holding her. Meredith clung tightly as their bodies met along their full length. The intimate contact sent waves of excitement racing through her. She pressed against him until the taut muscles of his thighs were digging into her yielding flesh, and her breasts were crushed against the solid wall of his chest.

Jeremy's body throbbed in an answering spasm that was evidence of his own arousal. His mouth became more demanding as he slid her body beneath his. Meredith's breath caught in her throat as he poised above her for a heart-stopping moment.

"You're mine now, and I'll never let you go," he muttered.

"I won't ever want to," she whispered.

His entry filled her with pleasure more intense than she'd ever experienced. It grew in increasing spirals until she was rocketing out of control. Jeremy was the sole fixed planet in her wild orbit. She clung to him as he drove her over the edge into outer space.

Her tense limbs relaxed as total satisfaction replaced tormented yearning. When their heartbeats slowed, he rested his head on her breast, and she stroked his hair languidly.

"It's never been like this." His voice was muffled. "I love you, my darling."

"I love you, too," she answered softly.

He lifted his head to look at her searchingly. "You didn't say that before."

She smiled enchantingly. "I thought this was an appropriate moment."

He rolled over on his side, taking her with him. "You don't have to say something you don't mean. I know you want me, that's enough for now. I'm hoping you'll come to love me in time." His face was troubled.

"I'm beginning to think you're not very experienced with women, after all," she teased. "You certainly never know what *I'm* feeling."

"I hope I gave you pleasure," he answered slowly. "But I'm talking about a more lasting emotion."

"You really do think I'm only interested in your fantastic body," she replied mischievously.

He smiled reluctantly. "I'm just glad I have something you want."

"Count on it!" Her laughter faded as she framed his face in her palms and gazed at him with eyes like limpid pools. "Darling Jeremy, it didn't take me very long to realize I was in love with you. I've been miserable at the thought of never seeing you again after you didn't need me anymore."

"I can't conceive of life without you," he said huskily. His tender kiss erased all of her doubts.

Afterward she sighed happily. "We must have set a record for misunderstandings in such a short space of time."

"But no more." He rested his cheek on top of her head. "From now on we're going to live happily ever after."

Meredith snuggled into Jeremy's arms, feeling utterly blissful. He was right. Nothing could come between them again. A pleasing languor stole over her as she thought about the future. Before she got past the wedding, her breathing slowed and she fell asleep.

For a moment before she was fully awake the next morning, Meredith thought the night had been another of her vivid dreams. But nothing in her experience could equal the reality of Jeremy's lovemaking. He had carried her to heights she'd never reached before.

He was sleeping with his head on her breast, still holding her close, although his body was relaxed now, rather than taut with demand. She touched his mouth gently, almost awed at the pleasure it had brought. He opened his eyes and smiled at her.

"I didn't mean to wake you," she said remorsefully.

"I hope you'll make a habit of it."

"I guess we have to get up," she said reluctantly. "I'll make coffee while you're showering."

As she started to throw back the covers he put an arm around her waist. "I'll make breakfast and bring it to you. I want to think about you lying in my bed."

"I thought you couldn't cook. Have you been putting me on all this time?"

"I had cold cereal in mind," he admitted. "But I intended to slice a banana on top."

She clasped her arms around his neck and kissed him. "It's the thought that counts."

He pulled her sleep-warm body closer, murmuring against her ear, "I have another thought."

"I'm not surprised." She laughed. "But don't you have to go to work?"

"Eventually." He reached under the covers and caressed her lingeringly. "Do you have to be someplace?"

"Not until noon."

His chuckle had a deep masculine sound. "We can cover a lot of territory by then."

The same magic was present that morning. Jeremy had a surer knowledge of what pleased her, and he drew out the delight until she almost begged him to take her. Their union was as explosive as before, a journey so fraught with ecstasy that she was drained when he finally guided her back to reality.

"I wish we could stay here all day," she murmured against his damp chest.

"I do, too, angel." He smoothed her tumbled hair tenderly. "How would you like to go away next weekend?"

"I'd love it," she said eagerly.

"Okay, you pick the place." He got out of bed and held out a hand to her. "After we shower, I'll take you out to breakfast."

"I'd better use the other bathroom in case Helga comes upstairs."

"She doesn't come in till noon." He pulled her into his arms. "I'll scrub your back like it's never been scrubbed before."

She drew out of his arms regretfully. "You can give me a demonstration next weekend when neither of us is on a schedule."

"I suppose you're right." He sighed. "I lose all sense of responsibility when I'm around you."

She gave him a gamin grin. "You're complaining to the wrong person."

The week that followed was the most glorious of Meredith's life. Jeremy called every morning, whether they'd spent the night together or not. He was busy on several occasions, but that didn't bother her. She was no longer tormented by uncertainty or suspicion.

Clara commented on the change in her. "You and Jeremy must have worked out any little problems you had."

"What makes you think we had problems?"

"It was either Jeremy or menopause, and you're too young for that."

"I guess I *was* a little hard to live with," Meredith said remorsefully. "I'm sorry I took my temper out on you."

"What are friends for?" Clara looked fondly at her radiant face. "As long as you two straightened things out, that's all that matters."

"You do like him, don't you?" Meredith asked softly.

"He's everything I've ever wanted for you." Clara's bantering tone had disappeared. "Have you set a date for the wedding?"

"I thought you wanted us to wait."

"That was before I got to know him. Take my advice and hustle him off to the altar before he realizes he could get a girl who can cook." The irony was back in Clara's voice.

Jeremy hadn't mentioned marriage, but Meredith wasn't worried. They'd had other things to talk about. She wore a perpetual smile, remembering his heated declarations of love—and the way he'd proved them.

It was Wednesday before Meredith got around to making inquiries about the weekend. Although Jeremy had told her to choose the place, she wanted to consult with him before making a decision.

"I didn't know if you'd prefer the mountains, the seashore or a quiet place in the wine country," she said as they were finishing coffee. Helga had made dinner for them at Jeremy's house. "You can take your pick."

"I'm glad you didn't make a reservation. My mother called this morning to remind me of my sister's birthday this Saturday. They're expecting me to join in the festivities." He gave her a resigned look. "She uses every occasion but Groundhog Day to drag me down there."

"That's all right, I understand." Meredith's smile was a little strained, although she knew she was being selfish. There would be other weekends.

"It won't be what we planned, but we'll have a good time. You'll like Phoenix."

She looked at him blankly. "You expect me to go along?"

His face fell. "Don't you want to?"

"Of course I do! I didn't think I was invited." Her spirits soared like a balloon.

"You're part of me now. I don't want to go anywhere without you—ever." He reached out for her hand.

They were gazing deeply into each other's eyes when Helga came into the dining room. "Can I bring you more coffee?" she asked.

After they both declined, Jeremy said, "Shall we go into the living room and let Helga clear away so she can go home?"

The corners of Meredith's mouth tilted in a secret smile. "I think that's an excellent idea," she answered demurely.

Chapter Eight

Meredith usually enjoyed meeting new people. She had a carefree, outgoing nature. But as the plane neared Phoenix, apprehension made her palms damp. What if Jeremy's family didn't like her? She'd heard that mothers, especially, never considered any woman good enough for their sons.

"Tell me something about your family," she said hesitantly.

"What would you like to know? I told you about my two sisters, Charlotte and Linda. Their husbands' names are George and Robert—not Bob." Jeremy grinned. "He's a bit of a stuffed shirt, but Linda loves him. I guess that's all that matters."

Meredith laughed nervously. "They might say the same thing about me—that I'm not the one they would have picked for you."

His eyes reflected the glow from the setting sun. "They'll love you almost as much as I do. How could they help it?"

"I hope you're right," she said in a subdued voice.

"You're not worried about meeting them?" he asked incredulously.

"It's a little late to think of it, but perhaps we picked a bad time. Your family puts a lot of importance on special occasions. You went home only a couple of weeks ago to celebrate one. Maybe they'll feel I'm intruding on a private event."

Jeremy's face was a study in mixed emotions. "That's nonsense," he replied, a trifle abstractedly.

"You don't seem too sure yourself."

"It isn't that," he answered quickly. "The fact is, something rather unfortunate happened the last time I was there. I had an argument with…uh…with Robert. It got out of hand and caused a lot of unpleasantness. We apologized to each other, but the matter is still rather recent. I don't think anyone will mention my last visit, and I'd appreciate it if you didn't."

"I won't," she promised. "You can count on me."

Before Meredith could ask what the argument was about, the stewardess came by with a tray of peppermints, and the captain's voice came over the loudspeaker giving the temperature and local time in Phoenix.

Meredith needn't have worried about Jeremy's family liking her. They were charming people who made her feel at home immediately. She and Jeremy stayed with his parents in a beautiful rambling ranch house that was unexpectedly modern.

When Meredith commented on how different their present home was from the former one, Mrs. Winchester said, "That was fine when I was a young woman raising a family. I don't need a two-story house or a staff of servants anymore. Now I just want to relax and hang out." She smiled at her son. "Is that the expression?"

He returned her smile fondly. "I think you mean hang *loose*, Mother, but we get the idea."

"I'm glad Jeremy kept the old family place, though. It gives us hope that someday he'll marry and settle down." Her remark to Meredith was blandly innocent.

Jeremy's father chuckled. "Like most women, Ellie disapproves of bachelorhood for any man old enough to vote."

She exchanged an affectionate smile with her husband. "I'm merely concerned with his health. Statistics show that married men live longer."

"Then you'll be relieved to know you can stop worrying. Meredith and I are engaged." Jeremy put his arm around her.

His parents' delight was echoed at the birthday party the next night. His sisters pulled her aside and welcomed her into the family enthusiastically.

"He waited a long time, but you were worth it," Charlotte said, giving her stamp of approval.

"I just wish we all lived in the same city." Linda sighed. "We had such fun when we were growing up."

"Don't get all misty-eyed," Charlotte advised. "Do you remember when Jeremy told your date you weren't ready because you broke your bra strap? You almost refused to go downstairs."

Linda laughed. "It's funny the things that embarrass a teenager. I got even with him, though. I hid his car keys the night of the junior prom. Dede Patterson's father had to drive them there and pick them up. Jeremy was mortified."

"I envy you so," Meredith said wistfully. "I never had any brothers or sisters."

"You have family now. Maybe more than you bargained for." Charlotte grinned. "Mother expects her little brood to rally round on every occasion."

"And you have no idea how often they occur," Linda agreed. "Let's see, what comes after your birthday, Charlotte?"

"We have a breather for two months until Mom and Dad's anniversary."

"But I thought—" Meredith stopped abruptly, remembering her promise to Jeremy.

"What?" Charlotte prompted.

"I sort of got the idea your parents just had an anniversary."

"It might have seemed like it to Jeremy. He can never keep his dates straight. One of us always has to remind him what we're celebrating," Linda said.

"It's time to open your gifts, Charlotte," Mrs. Winchester called.

Meredith trailed slowly after the others as they gathered around a table piled with gaily wrapped boxes. Her mind was working furiously. Why had Jeremy told her he came here for his parents' anniversary? He didn't need an excuse to visit them.

His behavior on the plane had been strange, too, in light of this new information. Had he really had an argument with his brother-in-law? Was that why he didn't want her to mention his last visit—or was it because he wasn't here? No one else had referred, even obliquely, to any unpleasantness, and Jeremy's relations with Robert didn't appear to be strained.

Meredith had thought her suspicions were a thing of the past, but Linda's revelation shook her confidence. What reason would he have for a pointless lie? Suddenly she thought of one that wasn't very palatable. Jeremy hadn't come to visit his parents as he told her, he'd gone away with another woman.

That was before they'd become *really* engaged, so it wasn't as though he'd been unfaithful to her. He was a virile man with normal male urges, she reminded herself. But it hurt, nonetheless. *She* hadn't been able to think of any other man since she met him.

"Meredith, this evening bag is stunning." Charlotte claimed her attention, holding up her gift. "You have marvelous taste."

"Of course she does," Jeremy said smugly. "She chose me, didn't she?"

"Anyone is entitled to one lapse in judgment," Linda teased affectionately.

Meredith managed a smile, but she didn't join in the general merriment.

Jeremy noticed her detachment a little later. "You're quieter than usual. Is my family too much for you? We can be a little overwhelming when we get together."

"They're all wonderful," she responded truthfully.

"How about me?" He rubbed noses with her play-fully.

"You're wonderful, too," she answered, but her voice didn't carry the same conviction.

Jeremy was quick to catch the subtle nuance. He took a closer look at her. "Is something bothering you, honey?"

"No, of course not," she said hastily.

He took her hand and led her into the den. "What did my sisters say to you? And don't tell me nothing, because I can read you like a book."

"I wish I could say the same about you," she said soberly.

"You can—or you should be able to." He trailed a forefinger down her cheek. "I've never felt closer to anyone in my life."

"Do you really love me, Jeremy?" she asked wistfully.

"Didn't all those nights in my arms tell you anything?" he demanded. "You've become part of me. You're a fever in my blood."

That described their passionate nights together, yet it wasn't what she was talking about. Love was a lot more. But when he took her in his arms and his mouth covered hers urgently, it didn't seem important.

The weekend flew by. As they sat around the breakfast table looking out at the majestic mountains in the distance, Meredith remarked, "I can hardly believe it's Sunday already."

"You didn't get here until Friday night," Ellie Winchester said. "Why don't you stay a few days longer?"

"We're not retired like you and Dad," Jeremy reminded her.

"But Meredith hasn't seen anything of Phoenix."

"I'll give her a whirlwind tour today," Jeremy promised.

That was what it turned out to be, since time was so short. She got only the briefest glimpse of Phoenix's many attractions—the parks, the lovely golf courses, only the outsides of the numerous museums.

"We could spend hours in the Heard Museum alone," Jeremy said. "It has an outstanding collection of primitive art, focusing on American Indian tribes of the Southwest. Their collection of Hopi and Zuni kachina dolls is the largest in the world."

"I'd love to see them," Meredith said longingly.

"If that's what you want, but we won't get much farther. I was planning an orientation tour to give you a general feeling of the area."

"I guess that does make more sense," she conceded.

"We'll come back in the spring when they have the annual Indian Fair. It's really interesting. You'll see Papago basket makers and Pueblo potters making baskets and bowls the way they did hundreds of years ago."

Jeremy provided a running commentary as they drove around the city. He pointed out the Mineral Museum where a fossilized mammoth tooth, a meteorite and one of the world's largest quartz crystals were on display. The Royal London Wax Museum housed lifelike recreations of famous outlaws of the Old West, and other museums contained equally fascinating bits of history.

"You're tantalizing me," she protested. "There's so much to see, and not enough time to see it. I feel like a kid in a candy store, with no money to spend."

"We'll get out of the car and walk around when we get to Casa Grande," he said soothingly.

The road to the centuries-old ruin wound through desert country rimmed by the distant Mazatzal Peak and Superstition Mountains. The flat, arid land was covered with scrub and punctuated by saguaro, eerie cacti that resembled giant hands pointing fingers at the sky.

"I can't believe we're only fifteen minutes out of Phoenix," Meredith marveled.

"Wait till we get to Casa Grande. You'll think you've been transported back in time. It was built six hundred years ago by the Hohokam tribe."

"I know Casa Grande means 'large house' in Spanish, but what is it exactly?"

"Originally it was a walled village. When the ruins were discovered back in the 1600s, only the tower remained standing. The man who made the discovery called it Casa Grande, and it's been called that ever since. The four-story building served as a lookout post with living quarters for eleven families, so it was, in essence, a big house."

The ancient structure rearing out of the desert was an impressive tribute to the men who had built it without modern equipment. Other evidence of an advanced culture were the irrigation canals designed and built by early farmers of the tribe.

A ranger took Meredith and Jeremy on a guided tour through the tower, and then they walked all around the village. When it started to get dark, Jeremy gently reminded her that they were forty miles from Phoenix.

"This is such fascinating country. I can't wait to come back," she told him in the car.

His mother concurred after Meredith voiced the same sentiment to her. "This weekend was simply too busy. We didn't even get around to discussing the wedding. Have you picked a date yet?"

Meredith and Jeremy laughed at the now familiar question. "No, Mother, but when we do, you'll be the first to know," he promised.

The following week was a hectic one for both of them. Several large conventions were being held in San Francisco, so Meredith's charter service reaped an unexpected bonanza. She was busy every day, but her nights were free to spend with Jeremy. Unfortunately he had visiting VIPs in town, and was tied up for several nights in a row.

"I could come over after I get rid of them, but I can't tell you what time it will be," he warned.

"No, don't do that. I know what out-of-towners are like. They'll want to stay out until all hours, and you'd have to get up even earlier than usual. The morning commute to the city is fierce." Meredith made the sacrifice out of love.

"You could spend the night at my place." His voice deepened. "I've always wanted to come home and find you in my bed."

Meredith considered the suggestion before rejecting it reluctantly. "Neither of us would get any sleep, and I have an all-day charter tomorrow. I can't afford to be groggy."

"That's for sure! I miss you, though, angel," he said plaintively. "Something is always keeping us apart."

"Things have to get better," she consoled him. "That's the way it happens when they can't get worse."

"And it's always darkest before the dawn," he grumbled. "I don't want platitudes, I want *you*!"

Meredith was resigned to the fact that she might not see Jeremy until the weekend, but the next morning her charter was postponed until the following day.

"At least it isn't a complete disaster," Clara said when she hung up the phone. "They could have canceled entirely."

"These things happen," Meredith remarked, trying not to look as happy as she felt. Now she could see Jeremy.

"When did you get so philosophical?" Clara asked with an arched eyebrow. "You're not exactly noted for your sweet forbearance."

"There's no point in getting pushed out of shape about something you can't remedy," Meredith answered serenely.

"My God, there's hope for Milt," Clara breathed.

Meredith laughed as she pulled the phone toward her to call Jeremy. When he came on the line she said, "How would you like to have lunch with a woman who's been worshiping you from afar?''

"Why not? I don't mind meeting new people."

"Just for that I should take back my offer."

He chuckled. "Why are you tantalizing me with lunch when you're promised to tourists today?"

"They stood me up. I'm all yours if you want me."

"When don't I?" he asked in a smoky voice.

"I can come over to pick you up, and we could...go somewhere." She was prevented from being more specific by Clara's presence on the other side of the desk.

To her surprise, Jeremy didn't jump at the offer. "I wish you'd told me sooner," he said hesitantly.

"I just found out." Her buoyant mood suddenly deflated. "I thought you'd be pleased."

"I am, darling! I mean I would be, but the...uh...the bank examiners are here today."

"Is anything wrong?" she asked quickly.

"No, it's just a periodic audit all banks have. They'll be here all day, though."

Meredith's romantic intentions were thwarted, but she was willing to settle for less. "I'll come over anyway. You have to eat lunch," she pointed out.

"We're having something sent in. I won't get out of the office all day. I'm really sorry, sweetheart."

"I understand." She sighed, cradling the receiver.

Meredith moped around the office for a short time, feeling let down. She'd really counted on seeing Jeremy, if only for an hour. They talked on the telephone several times a day, but that was no substitute for actually being with him. She'd settle for a few minutes if she could simply touch his hand and bask in his smile.

Suddenly an idea occurred to her. Even captains of industry took a break once in a while. She'd stop at the bakery to pick up some fresh doughnuts, and they could at least have coffee together.

Jeremy's bank was located in the financial district, an impossibly crowded area of downtown San Francisco. Construction on a new office building next to the bank added to the snarl already caused by too many cars and double-parked trucks.

Meredith's scant supply of patience dwindled as she inched along in the right-hand lane so she could get into the parking garage.

Two cars separated her from the entrance when she saw Jeremy's car driving out: The bright color caught her eye, then she did a double take. There was no mistaking his red Corvette. He was waiting for a chance to move into the stream of traffic.

Acting instinctively, she honked and waved frantically, which only gained her a truculent look from the driver in front of her. Jeremy was watching the traffic. A second later he saw an opening and darted out into the stream of cars ahead. Meredith was boxed in and couldn't change lanes.

When the light at the corner changed, he was forced to stop. She was able to follow him, but several cars back. As she trailed behind, Meredith finally remembered that Jeremy had told her he wasn't leaving the office all day. Why would he lie about a thing like that? He'd have no reason to. Something must have come up to make him change his plans. But he hadn't been willing to change them for *her*, a little demon reminded her.

Jeremy headed out of the financial district to the Embarcadero, where a wide avenue ran parallel to the wharves. Rusty freighters and gleaming luxury liners gave an exotic spice to the area, but Meredith couldn't spare a glance. The traffic had thinned out and Jeremy was taking advantage of the fact. The powerful Corvette was pulling away from her. He was certainly in a hurry to get wherever he was going.

Meredith frowned as she maneuvered to keep up. That was the kind of urgency she'd wanted him to feel for her today. Common sense told her to stop trying to catch him. He wouldn't have time for her anyway, and it wasn't exactly honorable to follow him. Not that she was spying, Meredith assured herself. This was one of the ways she could take to return home.

When Jeremy turned onto the approach to the bridge, the hard lump of doubt in her stomach dissolved into a wave of pure love. Jeremy was going to see *her*! He must have juggled things around so he had some free time, and intended to surprise her. If only the sweet dope had called first, she thought affectionately. At this rate they'd spend all their precious time driving back and forth on the freeway.

Meredith watched his car weave in and out with a smile on her face. His impatience was flattering, but she'd have to speak to him about his driving. Her smile faded when he took the Mill Valley cutoff instead of continuing on to San Rafael as expected.

She followed at a distance, no longer wanting to overtake him. An irrational dread filled her, but she couldn't turn back. All the suspicions she'd thought were dead sprang back to life, uglier now that she'd given him her love.

Meredith was afraid Jeremy might recognize her car, but he was too intent on his destination. He drove without hesitation to a residential area, as though he'd been there many times before.

The homes were all well kept up, with neatly tended lawns and flower beds. As Meredith lagged a full block behind, he parked in front of a redwood house that wasn't quite as affluent-looking as its neighbors. The signs of neglect were subtle: shutters that needed painting, grass a little overdue for cutting. Still, it was a nice house.

As Jeremy got out of the car and started up the path, the door opened and a beautiful blond woman came out to greet him. He took her in his arms and bent his dark head to her bright one.

That was all Meredith saw clearly. Hot tears filled her eyes, blurring the horrendous sight. She rested her forehead against the wheel as waves of nausea swept over her. The fool's paradise she'd been living in had turned into a Technicolor hell.

She drove home by instinct, feeling terribly fragile, as though the slightest blow would shatter her into a million pieces. Unanswerable questions besieged her as she parked her car mechanically, and let herself into her apartment.

In the safety of her own home she finally faced the death of her dreams. Jeremy had been playing games all along. He had never loved her. She'd ignored every indication because she hadn't wanted to believe them. He hadn't even had to seduce her. She'd practically thrown herself at him. How that must have amused him!

One thing didn't make sense, though. Why had he taken her to visit his parents? She could only suppose it was to reinforce the myth of their engagement. Introducing her as his fiancée would seem to show honorable intentions if she ever began to have doubts about the vagueness of their wedding day. What a shabby trick to play on his parents, though. Jeremy really had no scruples. He would use anyone to his own advantage.

What stories did he tell his other girlfriend? Did she think she was his fiancée, too? Was she the one he had been with when he had said he was visiting his parents, or were there other women? Meredith brushed her hair back wearily. What difference did it make?

If only she could get the image of them out of her mind, the passion they displayed, the urgency in Jeremy that she knew so well. Meredith shuddered at the realization that he had been making love to both of them, lying about his whereabouts to one when he was with the other.

The telephone startled her sometime later. She reached for it automatically, then drew back her hand. She'd have to talk to him eventually, but not now. Not while she couldn't trust herself to remain calm.

He would undoubtedly have some very convincing explanation. Jeremy was good at those. But this time her eyes would be wide open. He couldn't manipulate her anymore. She didn't care about his deal with Al—if there really was one. Nothing he'd told her was true, so why should that be?

Would they harm him if she didn't continue to play her part—whatever it was? Her body tensed at the thought, but she forced it out of her mind. She had her own salvation to work out. A future without Jeremy was too bleak to contemplate. Not the real Jeremy, of course, but the one she'd made up.

The phone rang at intervals all evening, but Meredith ignored it. She lay awake most of the night, trying to tell herself she'd get over him.

"You look like a rose that's seen better days," Clara remarked the next morning.

"I didn't get much sleep last night," Meredith answered curtly.

"That's pretty obvious," Clara murmured.

"Have the lunch baskets arrived?" Meredith changed the subject. She was flying a group of wine buffs to Napa where they would have lunch in a picnic area in one of the vineyards.

"Spike is loading them on now."

Meredith frowned. "I hope they're better than last time. We might have to change caterers."

The phone rang before Clara could comment. She answered and held it out to Meredith with a smile. "You two might try talking to each other while you're together."

That meant it was Jeremy. Clara obviously thought they'd spent the night together. "I can't talk now. I have to check on the lunch baskets."

Meredith left the office abruptly. What she had to say to him required privacy. Their conversation might also prove lengthy, although not if she could help it. But he wasn't apt to give up easily.

When she returned to the office, Clara looked at her curiously. "Jeremy said he tried half the night to get you. You weren't with him last night?"

"No."

"Where were you?"

"I'm a grown woman. I don't have to account for my whereabouts." Meredith hated herself, even as she lashed out in pain.

"I'm sorry." Clara was predictably hurt. "I didn't mean to pry."

"No, *I'm* sorry." Meredith ran her fingers through her long bright hair. "That was a rotten thing to say. I'm just edgy this morning."

"That's okay." The older woman eyed her obliquely. "This isn't the most tranquil time of your life. Little things get magnified during an engagement period," she said delicately.

This was the time to tell her the engagement was over, but Meredith couldn't face all the questions. Jeremy had sold Clara a bill of goods, too, so she would be on his side. Unless she knew the whole story, which Meredith couldn't bear to tell.

When she returned in the late afternoon, Meredith was drained. She'd been professionally cheerful all day, but the effort had taken its toll. The only saving grace was that she hadn't had time to think of Jeremy. Clara soon denied her that blessing.

"Jeremy left a message," she reported. "He put his people on the plane, and he's free tonight."

Meredith made a noncommittal remark and beat a hasty retreat.

She knew the sensible action would be to get the whole messy thing over with, but the prospect cut too deeply. When the phone rang repeatedly that night, she finally unplugged it.

A television program eventually lulled her to sleep, but the doorbell woke her up. She knew immediately that it was Jeremy, and just as surely that he wouldn't go away.

"Who is it?" she asked hopelessly.

"It's me. Where the devil have you been?"

"I don't want to see you," she said in a voice that would have carried more weight if it hadn't quavered.

"What are you talking about? Let me in!"

"Go away, Jeremy. We're all through."

"What the hell has gotten into you?" he asked impatiently. "Open this door!"

She had no other choice since his raised voice would soon rouse the whole neighborhood. With great reluctance she turned the knob.

He strode in, scowling. "What's going on? Why wouldn't you talk to me this morning, and why haven't you answered your phone?"

"That should be obvious. I don't want to talk to you."

"Would you mind telling me why?" he demanded.

Meredith took a deep breath. "I followed you yesterday morning. Does that answer your question?"

A wary look replaced his annoyance. "You followed me where?"

"Don't bother thinking up a good story, because I wouldn't believe you if you told the truth. Not that you ever have," she added bitterly.

He hesitated, thrusting his hands in his pockets and staring at her broodingly. "I'll admit I haven't been completely honest with you, but any lies I told were for your own protection."

"Don't insult my intelligence," she exclaimed angrily. "You lied for the same reason you made love to me, to keep me in a state of ignorant bliss."

"You can't believe that, Meredith," he said quietly.

"How can you deny it. I *saw* you with that woman!"

"Why didn't you ask for an explanation instead of convicting me without a trial?" Instead of trying to cajole her, Jeremy was sternly accusing.

"What more evidence do I need than what I saw with my own two eyes?" she asked in outrage.

"You can remember the nights we spent together, the ways we made love."

"Don't! I can't bear to be reminded of what a fool I've been. You think your expert lovemaking can make me forget those other nights? The ones you spent with her?"

His hands bit deeply into her shoulders. "I can't believe you could have so little trust."

"What do you expect, applause? I'll admit your sexual prowess is awesome. Not many men could keep two women that happy. Or am I underestimating the size of your harem?" Meredith was appalled to hear the ugly words coming out of her mouth, but grief made her powerless to stop them.

A muscle twitched in his clenched jaw. "Do you want to know who that woman is?"

"No! Spare me that much at least."

"Sit down and listen." He shoved her roughly onto the couch. "Her name is Diane Belmont, and she was the wife of my best friend."

Meredith drew in her breath sharply. "You don't have loyalty toward anyone, do you?"

"I said *listen*." His voice was ominous, but it softened when he resumed. "Everybody loved Bill. He was a happy-go-lucky guy who never saw any bad in his fellow man. He expected to be treated the way he treated everyone else."

The sadness on Jeremy's face distracted Meredith from her own misery. Suddenly she had a flashback to that same expression when he'd talked about a friend who had died tragically. She began to listen more intently.

"I don't mean to portray him as a saint," Jeremy continued. "He had his share of faults, but the only major one was gambling. All of his natural enthusiasm emerged when he sat down at a card table. Bill was always sure he was going to win."

"We talked about that," Meredith murmured. "A lot of people feel that way."

"But they usually quit when they've used up all their ready cash. The poker games with friends weren't any problem. If you play with the same people regularly, you usually come out about even at the end of the year. Bill's trouble began on a trip to Lake Tahoe. The thrill of high-stakes poker went to his head like three martinis. While the rest of us went to the cabaret shows after dinner, he stayed in the casino. Sometimes he played all night.''

Meredith was beginning to see the light. "At Big Al's?"

Jeremy nodded. "He held his own for a while, and then he hit a streak of bad luck. We all loaned him money, but he lost that, too. Finally we refused to give him any more for his own good. When the weekend was over we thought that was the end of it, but Bill had been bitten by the bug. He was sure he could win his money back next time. Even Diane didn't know he was taking time off from work to go to Tahoe to gamble.''

Meredith was unpleasantly reminded of the blond woman. Did Jeremy expect her to understand that he'd drifted into an affair with his best friend's wife to console her? That wasn't an acceptable excuse for his deceit. She didn't interrupt, however.

"The first indication she had was when her checks started to bounce. When she called the bank to complain, they told her their joint account was down to practically nothing. Their savings account had been wiped out, too. After she asked Bill for an explanation, he confessed that he'd gambled it all away. He was ashamed to tell her, though, that he was also deeply in debt.'' Jeremy's eyes were bleak as he walked to the window and stared into the darkness. "If he'd only come to me. I would have pulled him out of his mess.''

Meredith felt chilled. "What did he do?"

"He drove his car over a cliff."

"I'm so sorry," she whispered. Jeremy was obviously suffering the loss all over again.

His expression was formidable as he turned to look at her. "I promised myself I'd make somebody pay for his death."

She chose her words carefully. "I understand how you must feel, but gambling can be a sickness. You can't blame it on other people. God knows I don't mean to defend Al, but he didn't force Bill to gamble."

"That's what I told myself at first, until certain things didn't add up. Bill was a good card player. How could he lose *all* the time? I decided to investigate."

"That's how you met Al?" she asked slowly. "Not because of a business deal?"

"You're getting ahead of me," he said. "I knew I wouldn't get any answers if I asked for them, so I posed as a high roller. I'm a pretty fair card player myself, and I was on the alert for something, unlike Bill. It didn't take long to discover the dealer was cheating."

"What did he say when you accused him of it?"

"I didn't, because it still didn't explain how Bill had lost such a vast amount. There were table limits. I went along with them, making my regular contribution while establishing the fact that I was a banker with seemingly unlimited reserves." Jeremy smiled thinly. "You wouldn't have recognized me. Finally they made their move—the way they had with Bill. After they let me win a couple of hands in a row, the dealer said it was too bad the stakes were fixed. If I was playing in a no-limit game I'd have a chance to win my money back, since my luck seemed to be changing. He said there was a private game in the back room that he could get me into if I didn't tell anyone. I finally knew how Bill had been fleeced."

"Then how can you have any dealings with the man who did this to him?" she asked helplessly.

Deep lines were carved into Jeremy's face. "I took my information to the police, but they said there was nothing they could do without proof. I was ready to go after Al myself when the Treasury Department contacted me. They've been trying to get something on him for years. They proposed a sting operation, and I jumped at the chance. I've been working for the government for months."

She stared at him in a daze. "Doing what?"

"Al thinks I'm laundering money for him."

"Through your bank?"

"It's a perfect setup. I pretended to be in over my head. When he threatened me if I didn't pay up, I proposed a trade-off instead. You almost blew the deal when you blundered into one of our meetings. That's the reason your cooperation was essential. I had to convince him there wouldn't be any leaks."

"But why didn't you tell *me* the truth?"

"For your own protection," he answered simply. "Al wouldn't hesitate to take drastic measures if he thought you were a threat, and you're too honest to play a part convincingly."

Meredith stared down at her clenched hands. "So you made sure of a good performance by getting me to fall in love with you."

He dropped to one knee and raised her face to a level with his. "Our love will have made this whole thing worthwhile if nothing else ever comes of it. I love you, Meredith. Surely you can't doubt that."

She wanted to accept the whole story without question, but there was still the other woman. "You went to see Diane when you could have been with me. I saw you embracing."

"She's a dear friend. Do you really think a kiss on the cheek in public view is out of line?"

Had her vivid imagination supplied what her blurred vision missed? "You're evading the issue," Meredith said hesitantly. "We hadn't seen each other in days, yet you made time for her instead of me. You even lied to do it."

He sighed. "You'll never know how disappointed I was, but you said you'd be tied up all day. I'd already promised Diane I'd be there when the realtor brought a sales contract. She's selling the house because she can't afford to live in it anymore. The appointment was all set up. How could I disappoint her?" he pleaded. "She doesn't have anyone else to advise her."

The constricting band around Meredith's heart loosened at his explanation. "Oh, Jeremy, if you'd only told me! You can't imagine what I went through when I thought you'd been stringing me along all this time."

He looked at her with disappointment. "How could you have had so little faith in me?"

"It wasn't all my fault," she answered defensively. "You've been living a whole secret life. That doesn't show very much trust in *me*, even if you did believe you were acting for my own good. What was I supposed to think when I caught you in lies, like telling me you went to Phoenix for your parents' anniversary." That had suddenly occurred to her, and this was the time to clear it up. "Where were you really?"

He showed surprise. "I went to Washington, D.C. for a briefing with the Treasury Department. How did you find out I wasn't in Phoenix?"

The last piece of the puzzle was accounted for. She smiled enchantingly and clasped her arms around his neck. "You're not the only one around here playing cloak and dagger. I can be intriguing, too."

"You don't have to tell me that." His hand slipped under her sweater to caress her satiny skin. "How about a couple of friendly spies sharing their secrets?"

"You already know all of mine," she murmured.

He unhooked her bra and smoothed both breasts. "I need a refresher course," he muttered huskily.

Chapter Nine

Jeremy's lovemaking was even more inspired after this misunderstanding. In every way a man can please a woman, he tried to show his love. He aroused Meredith almost unbearably, then satisfied her completely. Afterward she curled up in his arms, filled with a warm glow of happiness.

"Promise you'll ask me about anything that bothers you after this," he said, rubbing his cheek against hers.

"Will you promise to tell me the truth this time?" she teased.

"Always from now on. I don't ever want anything to come between us again." He stroked her hair tenderly. "Just be careful, sweetheart. Al isn't a ham actor out of a B-movie. He's a very ugly thug."

"Stop worrying. He's finally lost interest in me."

"I wouldn't count on it," Jeremy answered grimly.

"It's true. The black sedan hasn't been around since we got back from Phoenix."

"He probably switched to another car. I'm surprised he didn't do it sooner."

Meredith smoothed away his frown with loving fingers. "All this plotting is making you paranoid."

His arms closed more tightly around her. "I'm not willing to take chances when it comes to you."

She twisted in his arms so she could look up at him. "Is there any danger to *you*, Jeremy?"

He smiled mischievously to dispel the worry on her face. "What can happen to a banker—outside of losing his assets?"

"I'm serious." She didn't return his smile. "What would Al do if he discovered you were setting him up?"

"He won't." Jeremy's expression chilled. "The hook is firmly set now. Al will be done in by his own greed."

"I've heard the term *laundering money*, but how does it actually work?" she asked curiously.

"In a variety of ways. One is to deposit it in a bank in amounts under ten thousand dollars. Anything more than that has to be reported to the government and accounted for. When a person makes money illegally, he can't name the source. If he thinks it can't be tracked down, he doesn't declare it or pay income tax on it. That's where the Treasury Department comes in. Evasion of income tax will put Al away for a lot of years."

"For failing to report less than ten thousand dollars?"

"No, for neglecting to mention millions." At her puzzled expression, Jeremy explained, "Over a period of time I've opened up untold accounts for him under fictitious names. As soon as all of his dirty money is deposited, he'll withdraw the whole amount."

"Why didn't he simply put it all in one day and withdraw it the next?"

"That much activity would draw attention, which is what he's trying to avoid. The operation had to be gradual, and thank God it's almost over." Anticipating her next question he said, "The sting will take place in two weeks. When Al comes in with his satchels to draw out the money, the T-men will be waiting for him."

"Does he have to know you were the one who set him up?" she asked fearfully.

"I *want* him to know." Jeremy's face had the sharpened look of a hawk. "This is the last thing I can do for Bill."

"I'm afraid for you, Jeremy! You said yourself Al is a dangerous man. I couldn't bear it if anything happened to you."

"Nothing's going to happen," he soothed. "After this is over we'll get married and live happily ever after the way I promised."

"Are you proposing to me?" she asked slowly.

"I thought I already had."

"No, we never got engaged actually. It was a matter of necessity."

"Only in the beginning—and even then it felt right." He lifted her chin so he could gaze deeply into her eyes. "You're the one I've been waiting for all my life."

"Me, too," she whispered.

When Jeremy's mouth closed over hers and his body made unmistakable demands, Meredith surrendered to her senses. What was she worried about? Their love was stronger than any outside force.

* * *

She was in such a sunny mood the next morning that nothing could faze her, not even the postponement of her noon charter until four o'clock.

"It's a honeymoon couple, and they decided the sunset would be more romantic," Clara explained.

Meredith squinted up at the sky. "If the fog comes in early they'll be lucky to see the instrument panel."

"Tell them anyone can see a sunset, but fog is a San Francisco experience." Clara paused to answer the telephone, then handed it to Meredith. "It's for you."

"Hi, darling," she said, expecting the caller to be Jeremy. "I was hoping you'd call."

A male voice chuckled. "Why didn't you tell me how you felt before I was spoken for?"

"Dennis? I thought you were Jeremy."

"You don't have to pretend," he teased. "I always suspected you were crazy about me."

"Head over heels," she agreed cheerfully. "But I'm consoling myself with Jeremy."

"You're a fickle woman, Miss Collins."

"So I've been told. What can I do for you, Dennis?"

"I called to ask a favor."

"Name it," she said promptly. Meredith thoroughly approved of Paula's choice.

"When you have some spare time, I'd like you to help me select a wedding gift for Paula."

"You're in luck, I'm free most of today."

"Great! Come to the Hall of Justice around noon, and I'll buy you lunch."

Even the traffic couldn't bother Meredith that day. She was indulgent toward the erratic drivers that usually infuriated her. Maybe they had urgent business somewhere. A little smile played around her lips as she realized how out of character her attitude was. But Jeremy's love made the world a magic place.

When she looked in the rearview mirror to change lanes, Meredith frowned slightly. Hadn't she seen that undistinguished tan car before? Jeremy's warning that Al might have had his goon change cars echoed in her memory. She relaxed when the other car failed to follow her lead and switch lanes.

It was a different man, anyway. She'd never gotten a really good look at the driver of the black sedan, but he was older than this man. The whole thing was making her as paranoid as Jeremy. She'd be glad when it was over and he stopped being so obsessed.

The normal congestion around the Hall of Justice was compounded by the noon-hour traffic. Meredith was too busy threading her way through it to think about Al anymore. By the time she pulled into the parking lot in front of the government building, he had disappeared from her mind completely.

The man in the nondescript tan car wasn't as fortunate in finding a parking place. When he finally located an empty slot, Meredith had vanished into the massive gray building. Swearing under his breath, he slammed the car door and went to a pay phone.

"I'm sorry, boss," he said after telling his story to the person at the other end. "I could go inside and look for her, but chances aren't good with all those floors."

"No, stay where you are and pick her up again when she comes out." Al had switched on the amplifying system that allowed everyone in the room to hear both sides of the conversation. After cradling the receiver he looked at the man sitting beside his desk. "Well, Manny, do you still think I was being too careful?"

"Don't go off the deep end, Al. She could be there for any number of reasons—to pay a parking ticket, or apply for a permit of some kind. She could even have been called for jury duty."

"Yeah, and I could be elected president of the PTA. It's possible, but not too damn likely."

"You really think Jerry is double-crossing us?"

"Not necessarily." Al looked thoughtful. "She might be taking him for a ride, too."

"But Moose says they've really got the hots for each other. She wouldn't pull the rug from under her main squeeze. What reason would she have?"

"Who knows? She could be one of those exposé reporters out to make a name for herself. Or maybe you're right and she had legitimate business downtown. All I know is, I'm not taking any chances. Not with so much at stake."

"What are you going to do?" Manny asked.

Al's thin lips twisted in a sardonic smile. "Jerry's been working too hard. Some nice salt air will do him and his girlfriend a world of good. Have the yacht ready to sail tomorrow night."

Since the bank was closed on Saturday, Al tracked Jeremy down at home the following day. It was late afternoon, and Jeremy and Meredith had just come in from playing tennis, when the phone rang.

"I didn't expect to hear from you on a nonworking day," Jeremy said, trying to conceal his annoyance.

"I like to keep in touch," Al replied with a trace of mockery. "How's it going, pal?"

"Can't complain."

"That's good. I like the people working for me to be happy. That's why I arranged a little bonus for you."

"What kind of bonus?" Jeremy asked warily.

"You and your girlfriend are coming on a cruise with me and the boys."

"When our deal is completed?"

"That won't be for a couple of weeks yet. I had something sooner in mind—like tonight."

"Tonight!" Jeremy exclaimed. "That's out of the question."

"Why?" Al asked bluntly.

"Well, I...we'd have to cancel some plans, and...and pack."

"You can pack now. The car will pick you up in an hour."

Jeremy's eyes narrowed. "How long would we be gone?"

"Just a few days. I thought we'd sail down to Puerto Vallarta."

"That let's me out then." Jeremy's tense body relaxed. "I have to be at the bank on Monday."

"Come on, Jer, you're the president," Al said jocularly. "You don't have to punch a time clock."

"I'd be better off if I did. You ought to know the head of the company works harder than anyone else."

"That's why you need to relax. I'm not going to take no for an answer."

"I'd like nothing better, but I really can't, Al."

"I get the feeling you don't want to go." The iron fist was beginning to emerge from the velvet glove. "Why would that be? You wouldn't be planning something stupid like a double cross?"

"I'd have to be out of my mind." Jeremy's brain raced frantically, seeking a way out without finding one. "If you're really counting on me, of course I'll join you."

"I'm glad you see it my way," Al answered with heavy irony. "I'll see you and the chick on the ship."

"Meredith couldn't possibly make it," Jeremy said quickly. She was standing beside him with a puzzled frown on her face. When she started to speak, he put a finger to her lips. "I happen to know she's really booked up next week."

"Her partner can take over. He's back at work now," Al said, confirming Jeremy's suspicion that everything concerning Meredith had been under surveillance.

"Have a heart, Al. No woman can get ready for a cruise in an hour. Maybe she can fly down later and join us," Jeremy suggested, playing for time.

"She can buy anything she needs when we get to Puerto Vallarta. Don't make me insist, Jerry." Al's voice was definitely menacing now.

"I'll call you back after I discuss it with her."

"The matter isn't open for discussion," Al grated.

"I said I'd get back to you." Jeremy's voice was equally adamant.

"What's going on?" Meredith demanded when he hung up.

"I'm not sure." He scowled. "It sounds as though something put a bug in our local gangster's ear."

"I gather he wants us to go on a cruise with him. That doesn't seem to indicate he's upset with you."

"It wasn't an invitation, it was a command." Jeremy stuck his hands in his pockets and paced the floor. "Why does he want to get us out of town? And why spring it at the last minute?"

Meredith's heart started to beat rapidly. "So we wouldn't have time to tell anyone where we were going? Perhaps we only have a one-way ticket."

"That doesn't make sense. If I disappeared, the bank examiners and police would be all over the bank. That's the last thing Al would want."

"Well, maybe it was a valid invitation. That would account for his sounding annoyed. I'll bet not many people turn him down."

"Not if they want to stay healthy."

"So it's predictable behavior for a man like Al. You haven't done anything to make him suspicious, have you?"

"No, everything's moving smoothly. We only have about a hundred thousand more to launder." Jeremy's frown deepened. "It wouldn't make sense for him to pull anything now, but I can't believe he has a sudden yearning for our company."

"What if we're looking at this from the wrong angle?" she asked. "Suppose Al is setting up an alibi. He might be masterminding some swindle set to take place while he's safely out of town. What better alibi could he have than a cruise with a respectable banker and his fiancée?"

"You may have hit on the answer," Jeremy said slowly. "It makes sense."

"But why the strange timing?"

"To catch you off guard so you couldn't come up with a valid excuse. He knows you can get away if you really want to."

Jeremy stared at her with indecision. "Even if your deduction is correct, I still don't like it. For one thing I object to being a pawn. But more importantly, I'm not taking any chances where you're concerned. You could also be wrong."

"I don't see how I could be in any danger. As you pointed out, Al doesn't want publicity. An accidental death on his yacht wouldn't be apt to go unnoticed. The tabloids lap up that stuff."

"It would also firmly establish his whereabouts," Jeremy reminded her grimly.

Meredith paled until she saw a flaw in his reasoning. "Al knows we're in love. He could scarcely expect you to shrug it off as merely a bad break if he dropped me off in mid ocean. He has to face the possibility that you'd blow the whistle on him. Besides, what reason would he have for wanting to get rid of me?"

"I don't know, and I don't intend to find out." Jeremy had made up his mind. "I'm going to call Al and tell him we're not going."

"I hate to see you do that," Meredith said hesitantly. "He's such an erratic creep. There's no telling how he might react."

"You won't be in any danger," Jeremy assured her swiftly. "I'll make it clear to him that it's my decision."

"I'm not worried about myself, I'm thinking of you. You've endured so much to make him pay for all the misery he's caused. Putting Al away is a public service. It would be tragic if he slipped out of the net now."

A vein throbbed in Jeremy's forehead. "I can't let him do that."

"Exactly. That's why I think we should go along with him. Tell your friends at the Treasury Department for insurance," she added prudently.

"That would minimize the risk," he admitted, although he was clearly torn between concern for Meredith, and his burning desire to stamp out Al's reign of treachery.

"There probably isn't any risk to begin with," she soothed when he showed signs of weakening. "The bad news is having to be in Al's company. But the good news is being on a cruise together. Does he really have a yacht, or is that as phony as the rest of him?''

"It could be a thirty-foot fishing boat with delusions of grandeur," Jeremy warned. "This is the first I've heard of it."

"Oh well, maybe he'll get seasick and we won't have to be with him at all." She looked at her watch. "I'd better race home and pack."

Jeremy's misgivings were evident in the deep lines in his face as he dialed Al's number. He didn't allow them to show in his voice, however. Restraining his anger when Al became coldly abusive was even harder.

"You took your sweet time getting back to me," the gangster snapped. "Who the hell do you think you're fooling with?"

"You sprang this on us rather suddenly. Meredith had to find out if she could get away on such short notice." Jeremy tried for a reasonable tone. He couldn't force himself to be conciliatory.

"Never mind the long story. What's your answer?" Al demanded.

"We accept your invitation with pleasure."

"Well, that's more like it. I was beginning to wonder if I made a mistake about you."

"Haven't I performed to your satisfaction so far?" Jeremy asked evenly.

"Sure, pal, sure. It was just a small misunderstanding. I got a little hot when I thought you were too ritzy to socialize with me, you being a banker and all."

"One who's in your debt," Jeremy reminded him cynically.

"Only temporarily. We're going to make a killing. You'll get rich on the next deal."

"You expect our association to continue?"

"Why not? It's a perfect setup. Besides, I look at a partnership as a sort of marriage," Al said casually.

"You mean we're joined until death do us part?"

"That's one way of putting it."

Jeremy's eyes were cold with disgust. Al was like a vampire, draining his victims dry. Once he got his fangs into someone, he owned them body, soul and conscience. Any punishment that resulted from his one miscalculation wasn't nearly enough.

"But this is no time to talk business," Al was saying. "We're off on a fun vacation."

"Can you give me an idea of when we'll be back? I have to inform my people at the bank. You do realize that, don't you?" Jeremy asked meaningfully.

"Absolutely. I was going to suggest you tell somebody where you're going so they don't think you ran off with the profits." Al chuckled jovially. "We don't want any bank examiners nosing around, do we?"

It was reassuring that he'd thought of that. Jeremy wasn't taking any chances, however. "There's only one problem. I can't get in touch with anyone on a Saturday, so I thought I'd write a note to one of the vice presidents."

"Good idea," Al agreed without hesitation. "Somebody has to be in charge while you're gone. After all, I have my money there." He laughed. "We'll stop by the bank on our way to the wharf and drop it in the mail slot so he'll get it first thing Monday morning."

Jeremy felt a little better after hanging up. Al hadn't raised any objections to having their whereabouts known. Jeremy wasn't happy about being his patsy, but Meredith's theory seemed to be correct. Al was establishing an alibi.

Jeremy's next call was to Steve, but he reached his answering machine instead. The message on it was worded to give information to the people who knew his real profession, without revealing anything to those who didn't. "Hello, this is Steve. I'm on a buying trip in the east. Please leave your message, and I'll return your call as soon as I get back."

That meant Steve was in Washington conferring with his superiors. Jeremy frowned. He'd wanted to discuss this new development with him. The department should be alerted to watch Al's men. It couldn't be helped, however. At the sound of the beep he left a terse message telling what had happened.

Al's yacht came as the first pleasant surprise of the day. *Lucky Lady* was a gleaming white luxury ship. Its elegance was in direct contrast to its owner, although Al was dressed as a millionaire yachtsman. His navy jacket over white flannel slacks had gold buttons with a nautical design, and he wore an ascot tucked inside the open collar of his silk shirt. The outfit was impeccable.

He might have passed for a man of breeding except for the vulgar amount of jewelry that bedecked his person. A large diamond ring flashed from the third finger of one hand, and an equally large star sapphire adorned the pinkie of his other hand. These were in addition to a gold watch with a diamond face, and a heavy gold chain around his neck that became visible when he loosened his ascot a little later.

"Well, what do you think of the old tub?" he greeted Meredith and Jeremy genially when they came on board. "Now aren't you glad you came?"

"It's magnificent," Meredith said. That part at least was true.

"I'll show you around," he offered.

He led them along the outside deck, from the aft section where the rounded stern was upholstered with gaily printed cushions like a giant sectional, to the prow where the pointed nose of the ship would cut through deep water with knifelike precision.

The main salon opened onto the forward deck. Except for the ocean outside its windows, the large room could have been the living room of an elegant home. Thick beige carpeting covered the floor, and fine oil paintings graced the walls. The period furniture was another mark of gracious living.

Al swelled with pride at their obvious approval. He guided them next into the dining salon where he gestured expansively with his cigar. "I can seat twelve in here with no sweat."

"How many of us are there on this cruise?" Jeremy asked casually.

"This one's only family," Al answered easily. "Just you, me, the little lady and a couple of the boys. You know Manny and Moose." He laughed. "Sounds like an old-time vaudeville act, doesn't it?"

After a look at Jeremy's set face, Meredith said, "Moose must be either very large or very small. That's usually the way people get their nicknames."

"He's a real hunk," Al said, slanting a sly glance at Jeremy. "You better keep tabs on your girlfriend. Moose has to beat off the women with a stick."

"I'll try to resist him," Meredith promised. "I wouldn't want to cause trouble in the family."

"That's the right attitude." Al's eyes were suddenly opaque. "We got a good thing going for us as long as nobody rocks the boat."

Meredith could tell she'd received a warning, but against what she didn't know. In an effort to get back on safer ground she praised the yacht effusively as they continued their tour. That part wasn't difficult. No effort at luxury had been spared.

"Do you have to hire a special type of decorator for a yacht?" she asked as Al showed them through the staterooms. "You certainly had a marvelous one."

"I didn't have to go through all that rigmarole. I took over this beauty as is. The only thing I changed was the name."

"What was it before?"

"*Indomitable.*" He smiled sardonically. "I figured it was bad luck."

Meredith gave him a puzzled look. "In what way?"

"The name didn't do much for the guy who owned her. He was a loser."

Surely he didn't mean that literally? It was inconceivable that anyone could gamble away a yacht of this magnitude! But in a crooked card game someone could lose enough to be forced to liquidate assets. Al probably picked up this beautiful ship at a bargain-basement price.

Their cabin, which he showed them to eventually, was more luxurious than any on a commercial liner. The room was large enough for a couch and a dressing table in addition to a wide bed rather than bunks. Picture windows instead of portholes would provide a stunning view of the ocean after they sailed.

Meredith looked around admiringly at the elegant furnishings when she and Jeremy were alone. "This is lovely. I was expecting a purple satin bedspread and mirrors on the ceiling."

"That's what you'd have gotten if Al had done the decorating. His decisions aren't prompted by good taste."

"That's fairly obvious," she remarked scornfully, indicating the suitcases that had been brought in by a crew member. "The least he could have done is offer me my own cabin."

Jeremy grinned. "It's the one thing I can't fault him for." He took her in his arms. "Having you all to myself every night makes up for a lot."

"I feel the same way, but that's not the point," she said. "He could have had the delicacy to let us make the decision."

Jeremy raised an eyebrow. "You expect delicacy from a man who wears more jewelry than you do?"

"I wonder what poor soul he cheated out of it," she said disparagingly. Meredith regretted the reminder when his eyes became bleak. "We must be sailing," she said hastily as the engines started to throb. "Let's go up on deck."

They stood at the railing watching the pier recede. A few people on the dock waved, and she waved back as the ship's horn let out an impressive blast. Gradually the yacht started to move faster. The distance to land widened until the towers and spires of San Francisco became miniaturized.

Meredith stared with shining eyes at a fairy-tale version of the city. "It's so exciting to start on a trip."

Jeremy opened his mouth to make a cynical remark, then changed his mind. He put his arm around her instead, gazing fondly at her rapt face.

"We're going to have such fun," she declared, carried away by the moment.

"I hope so." His voice was neutral.

"You're not still worried?"

"No, of course not." His smile was a trifle strained, but she was too entranced with the view to notice.

Al joined them at the railing, "Well, we're on our way. Next stop, Puerto Vallarta."

"I'm looking forward to it," Meredith commented politely.

"Can't wait to go shopping?"

"No, sight-seeing. I've never been there."

"You haven't missed much. All those Mexican tourist traps are alike."

"I understand a lot of well-known people have homes in Puerto Vallarta," she observed.

He shrugged. "To each his own. The place bores me out of my skull."

"How strange that you should choose to go someplace you don't care for," she remarked guilelessly.

Something flickered in his eyes for a moment. "Oh well, this trip is just for relaxation—a little fishing, a friendly card game. I figured we all needed to get away from the old rat race. Right, Jerry?"

"Anything you say, boss," Jeremy drawled.

Al gave him a narrowed look that didn't go with his thin smile. "Funny the way some guys have to be forced to take a vacation."

"You can't change a workaholic," Jeremy agreed blandly.

"That's where you're wrong. You can change anybody if you know the right buttons to push." Al's tone was almost openly gloating.

Meredith was worried about the tension she could sense building in Jeremy. "We'd better unpack before our clothes get all wrinkled," she told him hurriedly.

His face was grim as he unzipped his suitcase a few minutes later. "I don't know why we're going to all the trouble of putting Al away legally. I could drop him overboard and save the taxpayers a lot of money."

"Jeremy, you wouldn't!"

His tense body relaxed as he saw her shocked expression. "No, darling, I wouldn't."

"You looked so savage you frightened me for a moment," she said uncertainly.

He sank onto the couch and drew her down beside him. "You once asked me if I could commit murder, and I said no one knows what he's capable of under extreme provocation. That's true, but I came through the test. I've discovered I couldn't kill anyone—not even Al."

"The law will take care of him," she soothed.

"That's what keeps me going—that, and you." His eyes kindled as he gazed at her mouth.

She unbuttoned his shirt slowly. "Would you like me to help you forget your troubles?"

"I don't have any," he murmured against her lips while his hand cupped around her breast.

She pushed his shirt off his shoulders and unbuckled his belt. "Then you don't need me to do this?"

His chuckle had a deep masculine sound. "Keep that up and you'll see how much I need you."

Meredith continued to undress him, resisting his efforts to do the same to her. When he was completely nude she ran her hands over his body, tracing the width of his shoulders, stroking his tight stomach and rigid loins. When he attempted to grab her wrists she evaded him, moving to the throbbing center of his heated body.

"What are you trying to do to me?" he gasped.

"I'm showing you how unimportant life's problems are as long as we have each other," she murmured, leaning forward to brush her lips against his.

He clasped his arms around her waist and tumbled her down on top of him. Her long hair curtained their faces as he gazed up into her eyes. "I'll never forget again," he said huskily.

"I'll remind you if you do." She smiled mischievously. "And even if you don't."

Passion returned to Jeremy's face as he turned her on her side and unzipped her dress. "I never knew anyone could mean this much to me."

He removed her clothes lingeringly, pausing to trace the curve of her breasts, the gentle slope of her stomach. When she was completely nude he bent to kiss the white skin of her inner thigh.

"I want to make you so happy," he murmured.

"You do," she answered in a breathy voice. "Oh, Jeremy, darling, you do."

Meredith luxuriated in a bubble bath while Jeremy took a shower. The bathroom offered both facilities, plus a double sink.

As he toweled his hair dry after emerging from the shower he gazed admiringly at the captivating picture she presented. Below her bare shoulders, the pink tips of her breasts were camouflaged, but still enticingly visible. "You look pretty sexy in bubbles."

"You look even sexier in nothing at all." She smiled. "If we weren't expected for dinner I'd ask you to join me."

"I'd be willing to skip dinner." He sat on the side of the tub and played with one of the curls that escaped from her topknot.

"Our host is expecting us, and there's no point in aggravating him," she said regretfully.

"It would give me extreme pleasure to rattle his cage." Jeremy's comment was made lightly, with none of his previous tension, Meredith was happy to see.

"It's not nice to tease an animal," she reproved him. "Will the vaudeville team be joining us, or do they eat with the other hired help?"

"You and I are in the same category. Everybody works for Al."

"So you think Manny and Moose will be at dinner?"

"I'm sure of it. I'm only surprised they weren't dogging his footsteps today. This is the first time I've ever seen Al alone."

"Are they his bodyguards?"

"Moose is. One look at him will tell you that. He's a big brawny blond guy."

"I wonder if he was the one who was following me," Meredith exclaimed.

"I thought you said it was an older man. Moose is young."

"This was after the black sedan. Actually I'm not even sure about it, but it doesn't matter now. What's Manny's function?"

"He's a sidekick, a yes-man. I guess in gangster lingo you'd call him a lieutenant."

"Sounds like a charming evening. What do you talk to gangsters about?"

"I don't suppose you've pulled any swindles lately?"

"I convinced a man I was indispensable to his happiness," she answered lovingly. "At least I hope I did."

He hooked a hand around her neck and kissed her sweetly. "That's a sure bet in any lingo."

Meredith's interest in her traveling companions had been piqued by Jeremy's thumbnail description. She met them in the main salon where they gathered for cocktails.

Manny was vaguely familiar to her as the man sitting next to Al when she'd blundered into the meeting in Tahoe. He was a carbon copy of his boss. He looked like him, dressed like him and echoed all of Al's sentiments.

Moose was more a private than a lieutenant. While Manny agreed with Al out of expediency, Moose really believed his word was gospel. But what Moose lacked in brains, he more than made up for in brawn. His muscular body was even more awesome than Jeremy's, although Jeremy was more lithe.

Meredith was almost sure Moose was the man in the tan van. "Haven't I seen you before?" she asked when they were introduced.

"You got the wrong guy." He looked to Al for instructions.

"So many dames are after Moose that he can't remember them all," Al said indulgently.

"I thought he was the man who followed me on the freeway, but I must be mistaken," she said innocently.

"Moose doesn't have to follow women," Al said. "I told you—they're all over him."

"I can understand why," Meredith answered sweetly. "He's so articulate."

"What the hell does that mean?" Moose asked Manny in an undertone.

Manny ignored him. "I hear you're a pilot," he said to Meredith. "That's a funny job for a woman."

"I suppose you're right, but I'm so bad at cleaning house."

"She can't cook, either," Jeremy contributed with amusement.

"Looks like you've got a liberated woman on your hands," Al said.

"You don't approve?" she asked.

Al shrugged. "It's your boyfriend's funeral. Personally, I think this equal rights stuff is a bunch of garbage. Any idiot can see men and women are different."

Manny leered. "Yeah, like the French say, *vive la différence.*"

Meredith didn't know why she bothered, but she felt impelled to reply. "Physical differences simply cloud the issue. What's at stake are equal opportunities, and the freedom to follow our own pursuits the way men do."

"How about loyalty to the guy you're supposed to be in love with?"

What was he getting at? she wondered. "I don't see why one thing would preclude the other."

"Well, let's say you could make a lot of money in a business deal if you kept your mouth shut. Would you tell Jerry?" Al asked.

"I can't imagine any circumstances that would require that," she answered slowly.

Jeremy gazed at her fondly. "It wouldn't matter. Meredith and I trust each other. That's the most important part of a relationship."

"If you say so." Al exchanged a glance with Manny.

Conversation was difficult with the three men, but eventually dinner was over. Meredith dreaded the remainder of the evening, feeling it wouldn't be good manners to go their separate ways immediately.

Al wasn't bothered by such niceties, however. He seemed to have urgent business to discuss with Manny. They disappeared after a perfunctory good-night.

"Was it something we said?" Meredith asked Jeremy with amusement.

"I don't know, but try to remember so we can give a repeat performance tomorrow night." He laughed.

Chapter Ten

The cruise would have been idyllic if it hadn't been for Al and his cohorts. Meredith and Jeremy tried to avoid them by having breakfast in their cabin the next morning, and a sandwich on deck at noon. Dinner was the only meal they couldn't duck, but only one more of those had to be endured until they got to Puerto Vallarta. They were due to arrive the next day, which would offer an excuse to get off the yacht for a few hours at least.

As they cruised south, the weather turned warmer. Meredith and Jeremy were content to lie in the sun, alternately reading and napping. It was a rare treat for both of them to have no pressing business. Al, however, was bored.

"How about a game of gin rummy?" he asked Jeremy when he found him alone on deck in the afternoon. Meredith had gone below to get some tanning lotion.

Jeremy opened one eye and closed it again. "No thanks."

"How can you just lie there like a lump?" Al demanded.

"You're right, my back needs some sun." He turned on his stomach.

"Come on, let's play cards," Al coaxed.

"I can't afford to pay for the trip," Jeremy answered dryly.

"Cut the kidding," Al said impatiently. "We'll play for peanuts. You won't get hurt."

"I honestly don't feel like it. Why don't you play with Manny or Moose?"

"I'm sick of both of them, and I'm sick of this tub." Al jammed his fists in his pockets and stared moodily at the blue water rushing by.

"We've been on board less than twenty-four hours," Jeremy observed mildly.

"It sure feels longer than that," Al muttered. "How can you stand to sit around and do nothing?"

"Wasn't that the object of this cruise?"

"Oh...yeah, sure. But you can overdo anything. This yachting scene isn't what I expected it to be."

"You can always have the captain make a U-turn," Jeremy joked.

"No, we have to—" Al's attention had been wandering. He snapped back, trying to conceal his slip under a casual manner. "With my kind of luck I'd run into a traffic cop. As long as we've come this far, we might as well check out the action. Who knows, maybe the burg's livened up."

"It's a possibility," Jeremy answered in an absentminded voice. He was inspecting the other man covertly.

"Well, if I can't talk you into a game, I'll have to go see what other excitement I can scare up." Al seemed in a hurry to leave suddenly.

Meredith returned a few moments later. "Did you see any flying fish while I was gone?"

"No, only a shark."

She looked startled until comprehension dawned. "You've been whiling away the time with our host. What did he do to ruin your day?"

"It wasn't anything he did, it was something he didn't say."

She raised her eyebrows. "What language are you speaking?"

"Al was complaining about being cooped up on the ship," he explained. "I suggested turning around and going back, and he took me seriously for a moment. He said, 'No, we have to—'"

"We have to what?"

"That's what's bugging me. Does he plan to pull something in Puerto Vallarta instead of at home as we suspected? Perhaps I should have left word with Steve to alert the local authorities."

"Stop driving yourself up the wall. You can't stop him at this late date, but his luck is running out. Try to remember that."

Jeremy stood up and walked to the railing. "If only I didn't have this feeling that I've overlooked something."

Meredith gazed at his trim body with appreciation. Suntan lotion had given his long limbs the sheen of old gold flowing over well-coordinated muscles. She smiled at the secret knowledge that his brief white bathing trunks covered an equally milky strip of skin.

"I thought I'd given you a lesson in priorities," she said indulgently.

His expression changed when he turned and looked at her lovely face and slender body. "The subject was so engrossing I'd like to enroll in your graduate course."

She stood up and took his hand. "You're in luck. Class is about to begin."

Dinner that evening was about the same as the night before. Moose was silent, Manny said little more, and Al's boredom had put him in a bad mood—although Meredith had yet to see him in a good one. The brunt of keeping the conversation going fell on her and Jeremy, as before.

"You have a marvelous chef," she remarked to Al, seeking something positive to say. It happened to be true. The meals had been excellent.

"He ought to be," Al grunted. "I pay him enough."

She ignored the tasteless remark, turning to Jeremy. "Don't ever tell Helga I said so, but this chicken is even better than hers."

"Who's Helga?" Al asked.

"Jeremy's housekeeper. She's been with his family for years, hasn't she?"

Jeremy nodded. "She came to work for us right about the time I went away to college."

"It's rare for household help to stay that long. She must have been very devoted to your mother," Meredith said.

"Actually, my father hired her. Helga was working at the country club and Dad lured her away. She was the best cook they'd ever had. The other members were so incensed there was talk of throwing him out of the club." Jeremy laughed.

"You rich kids really had it tough," Al sneered. "Country clubs and maids. I suppose your family had a chauffeur," he said to Meredith.

She gazed at him with wide-eyed candor. "No, our family wasn't as affluent as Jeremy's. We only had one car and one plane, and we had to pilot both ourselves."

"Are you putting me on?" Al asked suspiciously.

"Well, maybe I am giving myself airs. It was only a used plane," she said deprecatingly.

After an amused look at Al's face, Jeremy changed the subject. "What time are we scheduled to arrive in Puerto Vallarta?"

"When we get there," Al answered cuttingly.

Meredith's temper started to rise and Jeremy's eyes glinted dangerously, but neither said anything. It was pointless to try to make small talk if Al refused to be civil. When the silence dragged on and it became apparent they weren't going to break it this time, Al became less surly. He even made a small effort at conversation.

"At least we're seeing some sunshine," he observed. "The snow's been fanny high to a tall Indian in Tahoe."

"The skiers must be enjoying that," Meredith answered, accepting the proffered olive branch, withered though it was. Why make things harder? She was rewarded for her effort. From then on the atmosphere was less volatile. They talked about what good time they'd been making, and whether anyone would feel like getting up at dawn to see their arrival in Puerto Vallarta. Al threw in the information as a further concession.

After dinner Meredith and Jeremy strolled around the deck for a while, then went to their cabin. They were both tired, as much from strain as from the fresh air and sunshine.

They went to bed early and she dozed off almost immediately. Jeremy woke her, however, with his tossing and turning.

"Is something the matter?" she mumbled.

"No, everything's fine. Go back to sleep."

When he got out of bed and started to move around the cabin, she opened her eyes again. "What are you doing?"

He had put on a pair of dark slacks and was pulling a black turtleneck sweater over his head. "I can't sleep. I'm going up on deck for a while."

She yawned. "Do you want me to come with you?"

"No, I'll be back shortly." He came over to the bed and stooped to kiss her bare shoulder.

The stars that had spangled the sky by the millions earlier were obscured now by clouds. But the hint of a possible storm had its own fascination. The limitless ocean wore a different face at night. It was so restless, so mysterious, home to millions of species of marine creatures, some of them unknown to man. Life-and-death struggles were going on under those phosphorescent-tipped wavelets, much the same as in the world above.

Jeremy stared at the dark water, feeling his nerves stretching to the breaking point. It was maddening to feel threatened without knowing by what. When would Al strike? How? What was really behind this trip?

When the questions kept going around in circles, he decided to do some laps around the deck. Maybe exercise would relax him enough to sleep.

His rubber-soled shoes didn't make any noise as he strode down the port side of the yacht, past the main salons and the galley, all darkened now. The ship seemed deserted until he crossed the stern and started up the starboard side where lights shone out of one of the cabins.

Jeremy hesitated, wondering whether he could walk by unnoticed. When he heard the strident voice of his host, he turned to retrace his steps. He definitely didn't want to talk to Al. A fragment of conversation stopped him in his tracks.

"—and Winchester's little slut, too," Al was saying viciously.

Jeremy clenched his hands into fists and started forward, then checked himself with an effort. He moved from the railing to the wall where he was merely a deeper shadow in the darkness.

"Who the hell do they think they are, trying to lord it over me? So their families were rich—big deal! They still jump when I say so."

"Why don't you just forget about it, Al?" Manny asked wearily. This had evidently been a recurring theme all evening.

"Are you telling me what to do?" Al's voice was ominous.

"No way, boss! I only meant they're not worth getting yourself so steamed up."

"I'll be the judge of that. No two-bit tinhorn and his cheap bimbo are going to make me look stupid and get away with it."

Jeremy's control was being sorely tried. His muscles cried out against the restrictions he was placing on them.

"They're the dumb ones," Manny said soothingly. "You've been pulling their strings, and they don't have a clue."

Al's anger was diffused somewhat. His chuckle held gloating amusement. "Winchester's about to find out what his college degree is worth. I'd like to tell him what he can do with it."

"If he was smart he would have figured out why he kept losing all the time," Manny agreed. "They never do, though."

"It's been a pleasure putting the screws on him." Al's black mood returned. "He's going to sweat plenty more before I'm through with him."

"Do you want me to take care of him when this is over, boss?" Moose spoke up for the first time.

"We'll see. It depends on whether I can trust him or not."

"I thought you decided you couldn't," Manny said. "Isn't that why we're keeping him on ice while you send the boys in to close out the accounts tomorrow?"

"Listen to me and learn," Al instructed. "Always take the other guy by surprise. Winchester expects the payoff to come down in two weeks, so we pull a switch while he's out of town. If he's leveling with me it won't make any difference to him. If he's not, we're in and out before he can do anything about it."

"Pretty slick, boss." Manny paid the expected tribute. "But we could have washed another hundred thousand if we'd waited one more week."

"Where do you keep your brains, in the seat of your pants? What's a hundred thousand when we stand to make over a million?"

"I guess you're right," Manny mumbled.

"Try and remember that. Do the boys have their instructions?"

"They're all set to go. I even told them to spend the night in San Francisco so they can be at the bank when it opens tomorrow morning."

"Good thinking."

"Will there be any problem without Winchester there?"

"He wrote a note leaving a vice president in charge." Al's voice held sardonic amusement. "I suggested he drop it off at the bank personally."

"You sure think of everything," Manny said admiringly.

"That's why you're all working for *me*. Maybe I'm not as educated as his highness, but I'm not jumping through somebody else's hoops, either."

"What about tomorrow when we dock?" Manny asked hurriedly before Al could get started on another tirade. "They'll want to go ashore, and there's always the chance Winchester will call his office to check on things."

"I think a host ought to be responsible for the health of his guests, don't you?" Al drawled.

"Yeah, I guess so," Manny answered uncertainly.

"Everybody knows how sick a person can get eating the food or drinking the water in Mexico." Al's voice was bland. "I certainly wouldn't want that to happen to any of my friends."

"You're going to keep them on the yacht?"

"Didn't they say how good the chef is?"

"What if they say they don't expect to eat or drink anything ashore?" Manny objected. "The girl is pretty keen to go sight-seeing."

"I'd feel it was my duty to try and talk her out of it. The discussion might last quite a while—maybe until late afternoon."

Manny laughed. "I have to hand it to you, boss. You sure know how to hedge your bets."

"It's easy when you hold all the cards," Al answered complacently. "And speaking of cards, let's have a game."

Jeremy hugged the wall, moving cautiously. His face was grim as he rounded the stern and strode back to the cabin. All the pieces of the puzzle were now neatly in place. He'd been outsmarted.

Why hadn't he guessed what Al was up to? It was no consolation to know he didn't possess the same devious kind of mind. The important thing was, the little thug was going to slip out of the trap. That was insupportable! Yet what could he do about it? Al had covered all bases.

Without thinking, Jeremy slammed the cabin door. He needed physical action to relieve his frustration.

"Jeremy?" Meredith sat upright in bed. "What's the matter?"

"Just about everything," he answered savagely. "You're looking at the world's biggest idiot!"

She brushed her long hair out of her eyes and stared at him uncomprehendingly. "You said you were going for a walk on deck. What happened?"

"I found out the price tag on this cruise." In short pithy sentences, he told her what he'd overheard.

"But that's terrible," she exclaimed.

"Tell me!"

"You can't let him get away with this."

"What do you suggest I do?"

"Alert the bank, of course. He can't keep us prisoners on the yacht."

"Who's going to stop him?"

"Well, I . . . the crew, for one." She brightened. "We'll tell them he's keeping us on board against our will."

"And Al will tell them his own story. Or perhaps he won't have to tell them anything. They work for him."

"You think they'd go along with this outrage?" She stared at him, thinking furiously. "Then how about this? There should be a lot of boats anchored in the harbor. Couldn't we call over to one of them?"

"You're clutching at straws." Jeremy jammed his hands into his pockets and paced the floor. "Even if we got a chance, who would believe us? It sounds like the plot of a television show."

"You can't just give up!"

"I don't intend to, but right at the moment I'm a little stymied."

Meredith folded her arms around her raised knees and watched Jeremy pace. "I have another thought. Al won't let you off the yacht, but I could make up an excuse to go without you—something like wanting to have my hair done. He doesn't have any reason to suspect me."

"I'm not so sure. That conversation at dinner last night was rather strange."

"You mean when he disapproved of my having a mind of my own? That's right in character," she said disdainfully.

"No, the rest of it. Al gave Manny a strange look when I said I trusted you."

"Possibly because *he* doesn't trust anyone."

"Including you. Besides, it wouldn't be difficult to figure out that I'd tell you to make a phone call for me." Jeremy ran his fingers through his thick hair. "How the devil am I going to stop the bank from paying out the money?"

"I have an idea," Meredith exclaimed. "Suppose you tell Al you don't feel well, and you need to see a doctor."

"He'd never fall for it."

She thought for a moment. "Well, suppose *I* was sick? I mean writhing in pain," she said hastily before he could raise the same objection. "Al might not give a damn, but he couldn't take a chance that it wasn't a ruptured appendix, or something equally fatal."

Dawning hope broke on Jeremy's face. "That might work."

"It *will* work," she answered excitedly. "He could be charged with murder if I died. He'll have to let you take me to a doctor, and once we're off the yacht we can alert the authorities."

"It's not quite that simple. Al would never let us leave without sending Moose along to watch our every move. Chances are he wouldn't let me go at all."

"It's worth a try," she said hesitantly, her buoyancy ebbing.

"You bet it is! I feel better already knowing you'll be out of danger."

"What are you talking about? I won't go without you."

"Yes, you will," he said firmly. "Once you're off the yacht you'll be safe. You can pretend the doctor said you needed to stay for treatment. If Moose tries to use force to bring you back here, yell your head off. He can't risk being questioned by the police."

"What do you think they'd do to you once Al realized we'd tricked him?" she demanded.

"Let me worry about that."

"You're out of your mind if you think I intend to walk away and leave you here!"

He sat down on the bed next to her and put his hands on her shoulders. "I'm not giving you a choice, Meredith. You don't know what these men are capable of. I knew the risks when I started this thing, but I didn't count on getting you involved. I couldn't stand it if anything happened to you."

Tears sprang to her eyes. "Darling Jeremy, don't you realize I feel the same way?"

"Nothing is going to happen to me," he soothed. "I simply told you the way it *could* work out. Probably Al will let me rush you to the hospital. That would be even better for us. They have security guards there."

Meredith knew Jeremy was pretending to be optimistic for her sake. His first guess made more sense. She was the only one who stood a chance to get away. Ordinarily she'd never leave him in certain danger, but this was her one opportunity to save him. The germ of a plan was starting to take shape in her mind.

"You'll do as I say, won't you?" he asked urgently.

"All right," she agreed.

He hugged her fiercely. "Do you know how much I love you?"

"I should by now." She drew back to frame his face in her palms. He looked so haggard that she managed a confident smile. "Don't worry, my love, we'll come out of this without a scratch."

"Of course we will."

She could tell by the desperation in his kiss that Jeremy had grave doubts. Could their life together really end when it had hardly begun? She rejected the notion violently. The plan would work. She had to think positively.

They spent most of the remainder of the night going over and over their plans.

"I think 7:00 a.m. would be a good time," Jeremy decided. "Al usually sleeps late, so he'll be groggy. We stand a better chance of catching him off guard. It also gives you three hours until the bank opens."

Meredith set her jaw obstinately. "I'm not calling them until you're off the yacht, too."

"We can't let him get away with the money."

"Let him have it! All I care about is you," she answered passionately.

"The money is incidental. Catching Al in a criminal act is the important thing. Think of all the lives he's ruined, all the people he'll go on destroying if we don't stop him."

"I'm not willing to sacrifice you for them," she said stubbornly.

"I'll be okay. After you phone the bank, go to the police and explain what's going on. If they need convincing, call Steve in San Francisco. He'll back up your story.

They'll take Al into custody, and we'll arrange for extradition."

Before the police closed in, Al could very well have killed Jeremy. Did he think that wouldn't occur to her? She intended to arrange for his rescue *before* she called the bank, but there was no point in mentioning it and starting the argument all over again.

"You'd better get some sleep now," he said toward morning.

"You come to bed, too."

"In a little while."

"Please, darling," she coaxed softly, knowing they could draw strength from each other.

After a moment's hesitation he shrugged off his sweater and slacks, and got into bed. They moved into each other's arms automatically, but Jeremy's body remained tense. Was he still going over their plans? Or was he thinking this might be the last time they would be together like this?

Meredith fell asleep eventually out of sheer exhaustion, but Jeremy didn't find that release. His eyes were tender as he memorized each of her delicate features in the dawning light.

A change in the rhythm of the engines announced their arrival in Puerto Vallarta. The steady throb of the generators slowed, then stopped completely. Activity could be heard on deck, and voices calling out muted instructions.

Jeremy slid cautiously out of bed and went to the window to look out. The scene that greeted him would have been romantic at any other time. The rising sun was touching the sleeping town with golden rays that gilded the old buildings and cobblestone streets. Separating the charming village from the blue water of the Pacific was a strip of white sand.

Other yachts were anchored close by, but they appeared deserted at this early hour. Even the crews responsible for them weren't stirring yet.

Jeremy turned back to the bed and stood looking down at Meredith for a long moment. A mixture of love and anguish filled his strong face. Finally he reached out and touched her cheek gently.

She awoke, instantly alert. "Is it time?"

"Almost," he answered heavily.

She sprang out of bed. "I'll be dressed in five minutes."

He stopped her as she started toward the closet. "All you need is a robe. You're supposed to have had a sudden attack in your sleep."

"I'm not going up there practically naked," she objected.

"You have to," he said reluctantly. "It wouldn't ring true for you to take time to dress if you were in terrible pain."

"Fortunately I brought along a nightgown for propriety's sake." She smiled faintly. "It hasn't been slept in, but I doubt if anyone will notice. Did you bring any pajamas?"

"No, but I'll put on a pair of jeans. It would be logical that I'd take a minute to dress, since I'm not the one who's having the attack."

"You're sure we should go up on deck instead of calling Al down here to the cabin?" she asked doubtfully. "Wouldn't that be more normal behavior?"

"Possibly, but he won't have time to think about that. I want to stampede him into letting you go."

"Letting *us* go," she corrected firmly.

"I'll settle for your safety," Jeremy answered huskily. He pulled her into his arms and strained her close.

Meredith didn't want to waste these last precious moments arguing, so she curved a hand around his neck and parted her lips. Jeremy was quick to accept their invitation, his kiss conveying a desperate kind of passion. At the same time, his hands moved feverishly over her body, skimming the sides of her breasts, molding her hips, curving around her buttocks. He lifted her into the juncture of his thighs, making her aware of his urgency.

"I love you so much," he muttered. "Don't ever forget that, no matter what happens."

She clasped his hips as he started to draw away. "I need more than words," she murmured.

"It's almost seven," he said uncertainly, powerfully torn.

She laughed softly. "An arbitrary number."

Jeremy's reservations fled when she stroked him intimately. He uttered a hoarse cry and backed her onto the bed. Meredith pulled him down on top of her and clasped her legs around him, arching her body.

"Love me, darling," she whispered. "Now and forever."

"There could never be anyone else," he promised as his mouth closed over hers.

His entry was exquisitely satisfying. She rose again and again to meet his thrusts, climbing in an ever-increasing spiral of molten sensation. They reached the summit together in a burst of rapture that was almost unbearably moving.

Meredith's spent body relaxed in Jeremy's arms as the aftermath of passion sent diminishing spasms of pleasure. Their love flowed between them like a golden current.

She stirred reluctantly. "How can I pretend to be ill when I never felt better in my life?"

He kissed her sweetly. "I know what you mean."

She sighed and ruffled his hair. "Well, fun and games are over. It's time to go to work."

Meredith was doubled over on a deck lounge when Jeremy reappeared with Al in tow. The gangster was in pajamas and a robe, looking bleary-eyed and confused.

"She was all right last night," he was saying. "What's wrong with her?"

"I don't know, but I'm afraid it's serious," Jeremy answered.

"My stomach," Meredith moaned. "I can't stand the pain."

"I have to get her to an emergency hospital," Jeremy said imperatively.

Al stared at her with uncharacteristic indecision. "Maybe it was something she ate."

"Are you crazy?" Jeremy thundered. "It could be a hot appendix. If it ruptures she could die!"

"You're getting all excited over nothing. She probably has an upset stomach from all that rich food last night. I felt a little queasy myself."

Meredith raised her knees and rocked back and forth, uttering wrenching groans.

"Does that look like indigestion?" Jeremy demanded.

"Calm down so I can think." Al frowned. "Have you given her anything for it? I got some antacid tablets in my cabin."

As he turned toward the gangway Jeremy grabbed his arm and whirled him around. "She needs a doctor, not a drugstore mint!"

Manny joined them on deck, looking puzzled. "I thought I heard a ruckus in your cabin. What's going on?"

"The girl has a stomachache."

"She has a hell of a lot more than that," Jeremy declared heatedly.

They all looked at Meredith, who continued to twist and turn in simulated pain. "Somebody do something," she begged.

"If anything happens to her I'll see that you pay for it," Jeremy said ominously.

"Okay, okay, I'll send her to the hospital." Al turned to Manny. "Wake Moose. Tell him to get dressed and get up here on the double."

As Manny disappeared down the gangway, Jeremy said, "She can't wait around. Every minute might count. Tell someone to lower the launch."

"When Moose gets here," Al replied adamantly. "She's not going to croak that fast." Before Jeremy could explode he, too, went below.

"Hang on, darling, we'll get help for you." Jeremy bent over Meredith, keeping up the pretense in case Al was lurking on the steps.

"As long as we have to wait for them, bring me some clothes from the cabin," she whispered. "I'll need them to get out of the hospital."

He nodded and left her briefly, returning a few moments before Al reappeared accompanied by Manny and Moose. The three men had set a record for getting dressed. Al had also alerted the captain, who was having the motor launch lowered into the water.

"Do you feel any better?" Al asked Meredith.

"I think I'm going to die," she gasped.

"Not on my boat you're not." He turned to Moose. "Get her to the nearest hospital."

As Moose approached her, Meredith said, "I want Jeremy to come with me."

"Don't push your luck, sister." Al ground his teeth. "I'm sending you to the hospital. What more do you want?"

"I want Jeremy," she insisted.

Al jerked his head at Moose. "Take her," he ordered.

As the big blond man hauled her to her feet, Meredith started to struggle. "I won't go without him!" Her raised voice had an edge of hysteria. "I'm afraid, Jeremy."

Two crew members on the yacht next to them had come on deck. They looked over at Meredith, cowering away from Moose. "Is anything wrong over there?" one of the men called.

"No, everything's okay," Al called back.

"You better calm her down," Manny said in an undertone as the men continued to watch them.

"Either you go with Moose or you don't go," Al snarled in a voice he struggled to keep low.

"No! I won't go with him." She took full advantage of the onlookers, making sure her panicky voice carried. "Don't let them take me away."

"Do you need some help, Miss?" one of the men on the other yacht shouted.

"Tell them to butt out," Al said menacingly.

"Not unless you let Jeremy come with me," she answered.

When she didn't reply to them, the crewman called, "We're coming over."

Al swore viciously. "Okay, you win. Winchester goes."

"Everything is under control," Jeremy called out, lifting Meredith from the chaise. She put her arms around his neck to indicate he was telling the truth.

"I ought to tie an anchor around both of you," Al fumed as Jeremy carried her to the ladder that led down to the waiting motorboat.

Jeremy had expected Moose to accompany them, but he was disturbed when Al and Manny followed close behind. "You don't have to come along, Al," he said. "Moose and I can take care of her."

"Forget it," Al grated. "We're all going. You're not pulling a fast one on me."

Jeremy gave him a level look as the small boat sped toward shore. "You're the one who is acting strangely. Is something going on that you're not telling me about?"

The other man controlled his anger with an effort, assuming a conciliatory expression. "Don't start imagining things. You know how excitable I am. We're all on edge over this thing."

"Sure, we're all worried sick," Manny agreed. "How you feeling now, girlie?" he asked Meredith.

"The pain is worse," she whispered, closing her eyes and letting her head loll back on Jeremy's shoulder.

"Well, hang in there, you'll make it." Manny shot a worried look at Al's grim face.

The hospital was only a short taxi ride from the wharf. Meredith was immediately placed in a wheelchair and whisked away to a private room while Jeremy was detained at the admitting desk. Al and Manny remained with him while he gave pertinent information, and Moose went with Meredith.

When the forms were filled out, Al said, "Okay, she's all taken care of. We can go back to the yacht now."

Jeremy thought swiftly. As soon as the doctor examined Meredith he'd discover nothing was wrong with her. It would be safer for her if Al wasn't around. Al would be suspicious, though, if Jeremy didn't argue.

"You don't expect me to leave her here alone, do you?" he demanded.

"Moose will be with her. He'll arrange for anything she needs. You'd only be in the way."

"She'll think I deserted her," Jeremy objected, knowing Al couldn't care less.

Manny showed an unexpected streak of compassion. "Maybe we could wait long enough to hear what the doc has to say."

Jeremy's heart skipped a beat until Al reacted with typical callousness. "I'm not cooling my heels around this joint for God knows how long. Doctors don't give a damn about anyone's time but their own. Come on, Winchester, we're getting out of here."

"They'll take good care of her," Manny said consolingly, but in a muted voice as they followed Al to the front exit.

"I hope to God you're right." Jeremy didn't have to pretend his deep concern.

Chapter Eleven

When Meredith realized Jeremy had been left behind at the admitting desk, she started clamoring for him. This time it didn't do her any good, however. Moose walked stolidly beside the orderly, who ignored her pleas except for a few vague assurances.

"I want my fiancé," she kept repeating all the way to her room.

If only Jeremy had insisted on accompanying her they would both have been safe. Her heart sank as she realized why he hadn't. If he showed his hand now, Al would have time to call off his bagmen. But there was another reason that chilled her even more. All three of their captors were armed. Their lightweight jackets couldn't conceal the telltale bulges from someone who knew what to look for. Jeremy was worried about innocent people getting hurt—a minor detail that wouldn't bother Al. She couldn't let them take him back to the yacht, though.

"Please don't let my fiancé leave the hospital," she pleaded with the nurse who took over.

"He'll be in the waiting room," the woman assured her. She stopped Moose as he started to follow them inside. "You'll have to wait there, too."

"I got instructions to stay with her." He brushed by the nurse and leaned against the wall, folding his arms across his chest.

"I don't know who told you that." She frowned in disapproval. "You can't remain in this room. I have to prepare the patient for examination."

He shrugged. "Go ahead, I'm not stopping you."

"If you don't leave I'll have to call for assistance."

Moose grinned. "You better call for plenty of it."

The nurse drew herself up to her full height, looking rather like an irate bird with ruffled feathers. She was a small woman, but in no way intimidated by his size. The doctor arrived at that moment and assessed the scene.

"Is there a problem, nurse?" he asked.

"This man refuses to go to the waiting room!"

"I am Dr. Cortina." He extended his hand to Moose. "You must leave these matters to us. That's what we're here for."

"I'm not telling you how to do your job. I just intend to stick around and watch you do it," Moose answered laconically.

"Unfortunately, hospital rules do not permit that," the doctor replied diplomatically. He was a slightly built young man with an intelligent face and a compassionate manner. He glanced toward the bed where Meredith was watching apprehensively. "I assure you we will take good care of your wife."

"He isn't my husband," Meredith said quickly. "My fiancé is downstairs."

"I see." The doctor eyed Moose thoughtfully. "May I ask why you're here instead of the other gentleman?"

"He got called away. I'm supposed to find out what's wrong with her and report back to him."

"If you'll wait in the hall I'll convey that information to you as soon as I finish my examination."

"I'm staying," Moose said doggedly.

Dr. Cortina's courtly manner was deceptive. Underneath was a determination more steely than Moose's. Without raising his voice he said, "We have security guards to deal with people who prove difficult. I would hate to have to call them, but that is exactly what I will do if you refuse to cooperate."

"I could break you into little pieces," Moose blustered, towering over the smaller man.

"I have many friends here who could put me back together," the doctor answered calmly. "You, however, would languish in prison for quite a few years."

Moose stared at him, looking for evidence of weakness without finding any. He swore impotently, recognizing that his bluff had been called. Having no other choice, he glared at the other man for a moment before heading for the door. At the last moment he turned and strode toward the bed. Meredith's muscles tensed, but his objective was the telephone on the nightstand. Yanking the jack out of the wall, he carried the instrument with him.

"Since you're so keen on privacy, doc, I wouldn't want you to be disturbed," he snarled.

The doctor and nurse stared after him in amazement. "Should I call security, doctor?" she asked.

"It might not be a bad idea to bring them up to this floor," he said mildly. Approaching the bed he said soothingly to Meredith, "Now, tell me where the pain is."

"There's nothing wrong with me except that I'm in terrible trouble," she said urgently.

He glanced at the closed door, then back at her. "In that case, why are you here? Shouldn't you be at the police station?"

"I can't go to the police. The men who brought me here have my fiancé. They'll kill him if I call in the authorities."

"Perhaps you'd better tell me the whole story." He pulled up a chair and sat down.

Meredith gave him a brief account of the events that had led up to her present predicament, stressing the direness of the situation.

"Al is absolutely ruthless," she said. "He'd kill for a lot less than the money that's involved here."

He looked at her doubtfully, confused by the condensed version she'd given him. "You admit your fiancé was engaged in an illegal activity with this man?"

"No, you weren't paying attention! He only pretended to be. The whole thing was arranged by the United States Treasury Department."

He continued to gaze at her for a long moment. "You'll forgive me for being skeptical, but your story is quite amazing. This isn't one of those television stunts by any chance?"

"Don't I wish!" Meredith said fervently. "I know it sounds unbelievable, but I'm not asking you to take my word for it. Call Steve Thompson at the Treasury Department. You can get the number yourself, and I'll pay for the call." Her eyes filled with tears. "Don't you see? Jeremy's life is in danger."

"Calm yourself, dear lady." He patted her hand.

"How can I when every minute counts? Please make the call."

"That won't be necessary. This whole thing is utterly astounding, but I believe you." He shook his head. "Who could make up such a story?"

"Then you'll help me?" she asked eagerly.

"If I can, but how?"

The door made a whispering sound as it opened to admit the nurse. "I'm sorry I was so long, doctor. That man is still lurking outside, and I wanted to brief the guard." Her pen was poised over a clipboard. "I'll take down your diagnosis."

"Not yet, I'm still getting her history. Would you check on the patient in 542? I'll call you when I need you."

"Yes, sir." She gave him a surprised look, but did as he said.

"Now, what is this plan of yours?" he asked Meredith when they were alone once more.

"I'm a pilot," she explained. "I can take Jeremy off the yacht with a helicopter if I can get out of here without Moose's knowledge."

"That should be no problem. I'll have the guard take him to the office for questioning."

"You can't detain him for long, and I don't know what kind of arrangement he has with Al. If Moose is supposed to check in at a certain time and he doesn't, it could be fatal for Jeremy."

"What do you suggest, then?"

"I want you to tell him I need an emergency operation. Say it's a ruptured appendix—we planted the idea earlier."

"You think he'll accept my word for it and leave?"

"Moose doesn't take anyone but Al's word for anything. But if he sees me wheeled out of here on a table, I think he might."

"It could work." The young doctor's eyes sparkled as he began to get involved. "We'll put you on a gurney and have you taken to the physicians' lounge."

"Wonderful! I can make my phone calls from there."

The door hissed open and Moose's querulous voice demanded, "What's taking so long in there?"

She slid hastily down in bed as Dr. Cortina frowned at the intruder. "You should have brought her in sooner. I have to operate immediately."

"What's wrong with her?" Moose asked.

"A burst appendix, from every indication. I only hope there are no complications."

"You mean she might cash in her chips?"

The doctor gave him an offended look as Meredith moaned softly. "Have you no delicacy, sir? I can only tell you the operation may be a long one. It would be foolish for you to pace the floor all that time. I suggest you go someplace more comfortable and return in a couple of hours."

"I have to make a phone call." Moose disappeared abruptly.

"He went for instructions," Meredith said after he'd gone. "Moose wouldn't get out of a burning building unless Al told him to."

"Possibly this Al will call him back to the yacht, in which case we won't have to go through such an elaborate ruse."

"That would be nice, but I wouldn't count on it."

"No, we can't do that. I'll go out and arrange for a gurney."

By the time Moose returned, Meredith's room was a beehive of activity. An orderly and a nurse were strapping her onto a rolling cart while Dr. Cortina made a great show of inspecting her chart. As they wheeled her toward the elevator Moose followed along, staring at her lowered eyelids.

"She's under sedation," the doctor advised him. "Hopefully she'll be conscious when you return this afternoon."

"I'm not going anywhere."

"That's entirely up to you." Cortina shrugged. "You may wait in her room."

"I'll be outside the operating room," Moose said doggedly.

"Are you sure you wouldn't like to assist with the surgery?" Cortina asked sardonically. "I'll get you a gown and a mask."

Moose didn't bother to answer. He kept pace silently all the way to the double doors that led to the operating rooms, where the doctor stopped him.

"This is as far as you go," he said firmly.

Moose didn't argue the point, but he watched through the glass panel until the little procession turned the corner and was out of sight. Cortina took over then and wheeled Meredith into the physicians' lounge at the end of the corridor.

"Now what?" Meredith sat up and looked at him blankly. "How can I get out of here with Godzilla waiting outside the door?"

"I didn't expect such devotion to duty," he admitted.

"Moose is more faithful than the family dog," she answered disgustedly.

"I suppose we could outwait him. He'll want to go for coffee, or at least to use the facilities," Cortina said delicately.

"Time is a luxury we don't have." She glanced at a clock on the wall, almost wringing her hands. "It's nearly nine o'clock already! The bank opens at ten. That only gives me an hour to make arrangements, drive to the airport and get Jeremy off the yacht."

"You're forgetting the difference in time. It's only eight o'clock in San Francisco."

"That's right." Meredith breathed a sigh of relief, which didn't last long. "That doesn't solve the immediate problem, though."

"How do we get Mr. Moose to end his death vigil?" Cortina asked speculatively.

They stared at each other, deep in thought. Suddenly Meredith's face lit up. "That's it! You've found the solution. How does a death watch end?"

"Isn't that what we're trying to determine?"

"You show him a dead body—mine," she said triumphantly.

"I'm not sure I understand."

"It's so simple. Moose was left here to see that I didn't slip out and go to the police or make any phone calls. If I didn't survive the operation, I couldn't do either of those things. He would have no more reason to hang around."

"How about making arrangements for disposing of your body, if you'll forgive me for being ghoulish."

"Moose wouldn't know how to get rid of yesterday's newspaper," she said scornfully. "Al will whistle him home and send Manny eventually."

"It does appear that you've thought of everything—except my reputation." He smiled. "I dislike losing a patient."

"You've gained a friend for life," she assured him. "I'll never be able to express my appreciation."

"I won't say it's nothing, because this has been the most exciting morning I've ever spent. Life will be very dull after you leave, dear lady."

"Your adventures aren't over. Will you do one more thing for me?"

"Anything expect perform an operation on Mr. Moose's brain. I disapprove of exploratory surgery."

Meredith spent a harried hour on the telephone, making her call with one eye on the clock. The request for help from the Mexican police was complicated by the language barrier, although they spoke English. Even so, they were reluctant to take her seriously. Without Dr. Cortina's help her whole rescue mission would undoubtedly have fallen through.

Even with his assistance she was cutting it terribly close. Meredith's nerves tightened unbearably when the clock reached ten, even though she reminded herself that was local time.

After all the arrangements were completed she said, "That takes care of this end. Remember now, you're not to call the bank until I return to the airport with Jeremy."

"I'll go directly there after I finish my errand," he promised.

"Well, I guess that does it then." She drew a deep breath. "I'm ready."

Cortina laughed as he arranged a sheet over her taut body. "I never knew rigor mortis to set in so rapidly. You make a very convincing corpse, my dear."

"Not if Moose could hear my heart beating." She swallowed hard. "Wish me luck."

"Rest in peace—and whatever you do, don't sneeze." He pulled the sheet over her head.

His smile had changed to a doleful expression as he wheeled her through the double doors to the outside corridor. Moose was lounging there on a hard bench.

Relief replaced his bored expression as he stood up. "That didn't take so long."

The doctor looked at him gravely. "I'm sorry. I did everything I could."

"You don't mean—?"

"The appendix had ruptured as I feared, and peritonitis had set in. It was too late to save her."

Moose struggled to deal with this new development. "I got to tell Al," he muttered, heading for the lobby. Suddenly he turned back, chronic suspicion on his face. "You don't mind if I take a peek at her?"

"No, I understand." Cortina turned back the sheet while Meredith held her breath. "Such a pity. She was very beautiful."

Moose stared at her for a long moment. "Yeah. Where's the nearest phone?"

After directing him to it, the doctor wheeled Meredith to an elevator. He beckoned to a passing nurse and said, "Take this gurney to 538."

When the elevator doors closed he went to the telephone booth where Moose was swearing at the marine operator. While the other man waited for his call to be completed, Cortina leaned against the wall and wrote busily on a notepad he'd taken out of his pocket.

He put it away and moved into Moose's path when the blond man came out of the booth. "If you'll step into the office there are some forms you must sign."

Moose looked alarmed. "I didn't have any connection with her."

"You brought her in," the doctor reminded him.

"I was just along for the ride. Her boyfriend is the one you want."

"I *would* like to extend my condolences. It must have been a shock, poor man. How is he taking it?"

"Okay, I guess. Look, I got to get going."

Cortina put a detaining hand on his arm. "Someone has to make arrangements for removal of the body. The hospital can't be responsible, especially with a foreigner."

"I told you, Winchester is the one you want."

"Then I'll have to speak to him."

"Yeah, you do that."

Cortina's hand tightened as Moose started for the exit. "I'm afraid I can't allow you to leave without some assurance that you or this Mr. Winchester will be accountable."

"Listen, you little two-bit punk, I'm getting sick and tired of you and all your rules and regulations!"

A guard at the front door walked over in response to Moose's raised voice. "Any trouble, doctor?"

"I don't know." He looked steadily at Moose. "Either you tell me what steps you're going to take, or you summon Mr. Winchester to do it for you."

"Al won't let—" Moose broke off sharply, staring at the doctor in frustration. "He's on the yacht, for God's sake!"

"Then take me to him. I'm not letting you out of my sight until I have him in exchange."

"Al would have a fit if I brought you aboard."

"All right, I'm a reasonable man. I'll send the police to escort Mr. Winchester here. You can leave as soon as he arrives."

"Are you crazy?" Moose looked at him in horror.

"Not according to our psychiatric department," Cortina answered calmly.

"Shall I call the police?" the guard asked, eyeing the large American dubiously.

"No! I'll take you to Winchester," Moose said hurriedly.

Al was pacing the deck with a ferocious scowl on his face while Manny jingled some coins in his pocket and looked worried. Jeremy's deeply ravaged face told of his inner torment. He stood at the railing staring broodingly toward shore. Their vigil was broken when the launch pulled alongside.

Al didn't pay any attention to the other man in the small boat until Dr. Cortina followed Moose up the ladder. "Who the hell are you?" he demanded.

"This is the doc that operated on the girl," Moose explained.

"Dr. Jorge Cortina," he introduced himself, holding out his hand.

Al ignored it, turning on his henchman furiously. "Are you nuts? What did you bring him here for?"

"I had to. He was going to call the police."

"What for?" Al confronted the doctor menacingly. "She was okay when she left here. You can't pin her death on me."

Jeremy elbowed him aside. "She's all right, isn't she, doctor?" he pleaded.

"The guy's cracking up," Manny murmured to Moose.

"He's the one who killed her, not me," Al insisted.

"Shut up!" Jeremy told him savagely. His fingers bit into Cortina's arm. "Tell me nothing went wrong."

The young doctor looked him directly in the eye as he chose his words carefully. "I know how hard this is to accept, but you must try not to grieve. Our loved ones continue to live on—in our hearts, of course."

"That's all we need right now," Al said in an undertone to Manny. "A religious pep talk."

Jeremy was staring uncertainly at the doctor, who reached for his hand and clasped it between both of his own. The folded piece of paper he transferred to Jeremy's palm went unnoticed.

"I did everything I could for her. You understand that, don't you?" Cortina asked meaningfully.

"I'm trying to," Jeremy answered slowly.

"You doctors are all alike," Al said disgustedly. "It's never your fault. Well, you can't nail me on this one. She was alive when she left here. What you guys did to her at that death mill you call a hospital is your problem."

Cortina remained unruffled. "I don't think anything will be gained by flinging accusations around."

"Oh, no? Then why did you come here if it wasn't to protect your own rump?"

"Certain arrangements must be made," Cortina said delicately.

"I get it," Al sneered. "You're worried about your bill. Okay, how much is it? You'll get your blood money, but you're lucky we're not going to sue you."

Cortina gave him a disdainful look. "I believe my business is with the gentleman concerned."

"I'm handling this," Al announced. "Just name the amount. I know you've got us by the short hairs."

"Cool it, Al," Manny advised after a look at Cortina's face. "This isn't Tahoe."

"Your friend is correct," the doctor said in a clipped tone. "When I said arrangements must be made, I meant burial arrangements. I shall require the lady's fiancé to accompany me to that death mill you referred to."

"Out of the question," Al stated.

"He is not free to leave?"

For the first time, Al appeared uneasy. "What kind of question is that? I only meant he's in no condition to hassle with a bunch of paperwork. The man has suffered the loss of a loved one, for God's sake! Don't you guys have any compassion?"

Cortina's mouth curled sardonically. "Perhaps we do tend to become thick-skinned. The dreaded paperwork must be filled out, however. What do you suggest?"

"I'll send Manny to take care of it." Al flipped a thumb at his cohort.

"Very well." Cortina looked at his watch, which showed twenty minutes to eleven. "I must get back. Can we leave immediately?"

Al glanced at his own watch. "He's expecting an overseas call. I'll see that he gets there by noon."

"Do that," Cortina said curtly. He put his hand on Jeremy's arm, his voice softening. "Keep up your courage, *mi amigo*. Help comes from unexpected sources."

Al watched with a sullen expression as the motorboat pulled away. "You'd think the jerk was a preacher instead of a doctor."

"I'm going down to my cabin," Jeremy said abruptly.

"Is there anything I can do for you?" Manny asked awkwardly. "You want to take a bottle with you?"

"No, I'll be all right. I just want to be alone for a while."

Manny watched him go. "Poor guy. He must feel like he just rolled snake eyes."

"Yeah, it's a bummer." Al seemed more put out than saddened. "But it could have been worse. If she'd cashed in her chips here on board we'd have been in a hell of a mess. To be on the safe side we'd better blow this joint as soon as I get word from the boys. Tell the captain to be ready to shove off."

Below in his cabin, Jeremy breathed a sigh of relief as he read and reread the note Cortina had given him.

Meredith had been undergoing her own trauma at the hospital. After she finally got back to her room she dressed hurriedly, reflecting on the scene in the elevator. At any other time it would have been hilarious. When she sat up on the table, the nurse had fainted and another woman had become hysterical. To add to the confusion a man had pushed the emergency button, stranding them between floors. What he thought that would accomplish she couldn't imagine. Precious time had been wasted while she got the elevator started again, meanwhile trying to explain to the passengers that they weren't having a religious experience.

"One thing is for sure," she muttered, zipping her jeans hastily. "I'll never be able to come back to Puerto Vallarta again."

The taxi ride to the airport would have turned her hair gray at any other time, but Meredith welcomed the breakneck speed. Time was ticking away inexorably. Had the doctor been able to convince Moose to take him to the yacht? Would the police show up too soon or too late? Could she get to Jeremy in time?

She reached the airport with fourteen minutes to spare. Finding the helicopter office shaved off several of them, but luckily it was located on the field where their choppers were hangared. Her spirits soared—until she ran headlong into a solid wall of bureaucracy.

"Yes, the police contacted us." The woman at the desk smiled encouragingly. "They instructed us to put a helicopter at your disposal. It's waiting on the field."

"Thank the Lord," Meredith breathed.

"May I see your pilot's license?"

"I don't have it with me." Meredith was still panting from her dash through the airport. "I'll bring it to you later."

The woman's smile dimmed. "We're required to have a record of your license number on file."

"I'm familiar with regulations, but this is a special circumstance."

"We're not permitted to make exceptions," the woman said stubbornly.

Meredith glared at her in outrage. "I have clearance from the police! What more do you want?"

"Your license," the woman answered adamantly.

Meredith almost had a full-blown tantrum, until she realized it wouldn't accomplish anything. Besides, a glance at the wall clock told her she couldn't afford the luxury.

She forced the urgency out of her voice. "Dr. Cortina will be along with it shortly. I'm sure you're familiar with him. He's head surgeon at your Lady of Mercy Hospital." Whether he was or not, this woman wasn't likely to know.

"He has your license?" The woman appeared confused.

"I left it in my hotel room. Wasn't that careless of me? But Dr. Cortina is such a dear friend. He volunteered to bring it to me." Meredith glanced out at the field. "Is that my helicopter?"

"When your papers are in order."

"Goodness! That doesn't look like the ones I'm used to." Meredith bit her lip in perplexity. "Maybe I'd better take a look at it. I might have made this whole trip out here for nothing."

The woman was definitely worried now. "I was told you were a licensed pilot."

"On Sikorskys, yes, but that looks like a Grumman," Meredith improvised. "I wouldn't consider taking one of those up."

The woman stared after her doubtfully as Meredith walked out to the helicopter at a normal pace, instead of running as every impulse urged her to do. She inspected the outside with her hands on her hips, before climbing leisurely into the cockpit. Once inside she was galvanized. A flip of a switch activated the rotors, and the chopper lifted off in a rush of wind.

After a moment of stunned surprise, several people rushed toward the helipad. Their shouts were drowned out by the noise of the motor, and Meredith ignored their wildly waving arms. Her full attention was focused on the blue water visible in the distance.

Lucky Lady was easy to locate. It rode regally at anchor, lording it over its neighbors in both size and luxury. As she drew nearer she saw a large launch pulled up alongside. The police were already there!

Several men were having a dialogue with the occupants of the yacht. Meredith's heart leaped with joy as she made out Jeremy's dear, familiar frame among the other three men.

Her elation was immediately replaced by concern. Hadn't Dr. Cortina been able to get aboard the yacht? The note he was supposed to deliver told Jeremy to go to the stern of the ship. He must be safe now, though. Al wouldn't dare harm him in full view of the police. She hovered over the scene like a giant dragonfly, frustrated at not knowing what was taking place below.

Al was experiencing even stronger emotions. The police boat had come as a nasty surprise. When one of the men announced their identity, he naturally thought they were there in connection with Meredith's "death." Being detained for an investigation was the last thing he wanted at that time.

"We're coming aboard," the lieutenant announced.

Al took immediate offense at his officious manner. "This is an American ship, buster. Nobody comes on board unless I say so."

"You are in Mexican waters, *señor*. We will board by force if we have to."

"For God's sake, Al, let them on before they start shooting," Manny urged. "You know how excitable these people are."

"I'll make them sorry they ever tangled with *me*!" Al leaned over the railing. "You don't scare me. I'm an American citizen. Try anything funny and you're in big trouble."

Jeremy was part of the small group on deck when the police boat pulled up. He'd come up from the cabin a short time before, and Al had compelled him to join them, overriding his plea that he wanted to be alone. Now that Al's attention was diverted, Jeremy started to drift away unobtrusively. He hadn't reckoned with Al's bodyguard, however.

Moose put out a restraining arm. "Where do you think you're going?"

"I've heard Al's tirades before," Jeremy answered contemptuously.

"It won't hurt to stick around for another one."

"Give me one good reason."

"Because I said so," Moose replied insolently.

Jeremy's fists clenched, but he couldn't indulge his long-standing desire to punch the thug's lights out. Not then, at least. It was a promise he made to himself for the future.

"This is your last chance, *señor*," the police lieutenant was saying.

Manny pushed Al aside, a mark of his desperation. "That doctor was lying if he said we had anything to do with the girl's death."

The officer's upturned face was puzzled. "What girl is that, *señor*?"

"Isn't that what you're here about?"

"We have a request to detain you for questioning."

"You're crazy," Al snarled. "I'm not wanted for anything. Nobody even knows I'm here. Unless—" He whirled around and stared at Jeremy. "You blew the whistle, you lousy stoolie!"

Jeremy stole a glance at the circling helicopter. "You're not thinking clearly. Why would I do a thing like that? I have as much to lose as you do."

"You have a lot more." The gangster's eyes were narrow slits of rage. "Take him below," he ordered Moose. "I'll deal with him later. Manny, tell the captain to get this bucket of bolts out of here, *now*!"

When scraping noises sounded on the side of the yacht, Manny lost his nerve. "Don't be a fool! The place is crawling with cops. It will be Jerry's word against ours. They don't have anything on us."

"Maybe you want to rot in prison, but I don't." Al turned back to the railing, revolver in hand. "Okay, hold it right there, or I'll blow your head off."

As soon as Al turned away, Jeremy sprinted for the stern of the ship. Moose reacted instantly and raced after him, but Jeremy had a crucial moment's advantage.

With the police alongside the yacht, Meredith had thought the crisis was over. But seeing Jeremy break for the stern with Moose in hot pursuit told her the situation was still critical. She gunned her motor and sped to the rear of the ship. Descending straight down, she dropped a ladder over the side of the helicopter.

Jeremy had almost reached it when Moose grabbed him from behind. The two men grappled while Meredith waited helplessly, keeping the chopper in position.

The outcome could go either way, she realized despairingly. They were both powerful men in top condition. She watched them batter each other, wincing with every blow. Jeremy had a secret weapon, however. His pent-up fury gave him almost superhuman strength. The short battle came to an end with a savage uppercut that sent Moose sprawling on the deck.

He recovered quickly, though, making a lunge for Jeremy as he grabbed the ladder. Meredith lifted him out of Moose's reach, but she was afraid to take off until he was securely inside the helicopter. That was what she was forced to do, however, when Moose drew his gun.

She swung out over the ocean, saying a silent prayer that she could get out of Moose's range without dislodging Jeremy from his precarious perch. When his head appeared in her vision and he climbed into the passenger seat, she was almost dizzy with relief.

"Are you all right?" they both asked simultaneously.

"Oh, Jeremy darling, I was never so scared in my life!"

"How do you think I felt when they told me you were dead?" He gripped her knee convulsively, as though to make sure she was real. "What happened? That wasn't part of the plan."

She laughed a little giddily. "I had to improvise." She gave him a sketchy account of the events at the hospital.

"I've put you through so much," he said remorsefully.

"Don't think it won't cost you." She looked at him with pure love. "From now on I expect to live happily ever after like you promised."

"I guarantee it," he said huskily. "Will you take this eggbeater down so I can make love to you?"

Jeremy's plans were thwarted when they were greeted by police at the airport. A lot of loud voices were raised, and much time consumed before Meredith was cleared of theft charges. It took Dr. Cortina to straighten things out.

"How can we ever thank you?" she asked the doctor after she'd finally been released by the police.

"You can go home, so I can get back to treating sick people," he joked.

"No reflection on your beautiful country, but that's our dearest wish," Jeremy said fervently.

"May I make a suggestion? You've both been through a traumatic experience. Why don't you stay overnight and fly home tomorrow?"

"We do have to go back to the yacht for our things," Meredith said. "Al and his henchmen are gone, aren't they?" she asked Cortina.

He nodded. "They've been taken into custody. The other charges against them would have been sufficient, but shooting a hole in a police boat guaranteed matters."

"Well then, since we've paid quite a lot for this trip, we might as well get our money's worth." Meredith smiled.

Jeremy winced. "It's a terrible thing for a banker to say, but I don't want to hear the word *money* again."

Two long distance telephone calls to Steve and the bank vice president had put Jeremy's mind at rest. Al's bagmen were in custody, and Steve was already processing extradition papers for Al and his vaudeville team.

The status of the yacht was in limbo, so the captain was delighted to see them return. Since the captain and crew were only employees, Jeremy told the captain he'd use his influence to get permission for them all to return home as soon as possible. The gratitude of the crew was immediate. Meredith and Jeremy felt as though they were aboard their own private yacht as they dined on deck under the stars.

"I could get used to this," she said dreamily, gazing at the lights of Puerto Vallarta reflected in the dark water.

"It would be bad for my image." Jeremy chuckled. "My depositors might think I was dipping into the till."

"You could tell them you picked up small change by running a Laundromat on the side," she teased.

Some of the strain returned to his face as he leaned forward and covered her hand with his. "I'll never forgive myself for putting you in danger."

"You couldn't know, and I'm glad I was part of avenging your friend." She smiled to lighten the serious mood. "We work well together. Do you think we're in the wrong business? Maybe we should become crusaders for justice like Superman and Lois Lane, or Batman and Robin."

He returned her smile ruefully. "I don't think my ego could take it. You were the one who rode to the rescue."

"Only because I was more mobile." She gazed at him with love. "You have considerable expertise in other fields."

"Could you be more specific?" Pinpoints of light reflected in his eyes.

"Not here," she murmured.

They walked down the stairs holding hands. Inside the cabin Jeremy took her in his arms and kissed her with great tenderness.

They made love slowly, with none of the desperation of the last time. This was a celebration of the senses, a joyful union that reaffirmed their deep commitment. Afterward they lay spent in each other's arms, replete with pleasure. Jeremy's gentle caresses over the length of her body were an extension of that pleasure.

As his fingertips feathered over her breasts he murmured, "I've been thinking about our wedding. Are you really that crazy about daffodils?"

She smiled. "They were your choice. I can take them or leave them."

"That's good, because I can't wait until spring to get married."

"I believe I can find a free day next week. This happens to be our slow season."

"Not after you get your new helicopter."

Her smile faded. "I don't think it's a good idea for your bank to loan me money."

"I don't, either." He nibbled on her ear. "Have I ever told you what delectable earlobes you have?"

"Jeremy, stop! We have to get this settled. I can't accept a loan."

"I didn't think you would. But you can't refuse a wedding present."

She sat up in bed and stared at him, wide-eyed. "Do you know what helicopters cost?"

He chuckled, drawing her back into his arms. "You're marrying a very rich man, angel, thanks to my laundry business."

"But you didn't get to keep any of it."

"I got something more precious than money." He looked at her with deep emotion. "I won you."

As Meredith melted into his embrace, she knew they had both gambled and won.

* * * * *

Silhouette Special Edition

MORE SPECIAL THAN EVER,
SAY THESE TOP AUTHORS:

JO ANN ALGERMISSEN

"To me, writing—or reading—a Silhouette Special Edition *is* special. Longer, deeper, more emotionally involving than many romances, 'Specials' allow me to climb inside the hearts of my characters. I personally struggle with each of their problems, sympathize with the heroine, and almost fall in love with the hero myself! What I truly enjoy is knowing that the commitment between the hero and heroine will be as lasting as my own marriage—forever. That's special."

TRACY SINCLAIR

"I hope everyone enjoys reading Silhouette Special Editions as much as I enjoy writing them. The world of romance is a magic place where dreams come true. I love to travel to glamorous locales with my characters and share in the excitement that fills their lives. These people become real to me. I laugh and cry with them; I rejoice in their ultimate happiness. I am also reluctant to see the adventure end because I am having such a good time. That's what makes these books so special to me—and, I hope, to you."

SSE-A2

Silhouette Desire®

1989
IS THE YEAR
OF THE MAN!

What makes a romance? A special man, of course, and Silhouette Desire celebrates that fact with *twelve* of them! From Mr. January to Mr. December, every month has a tribute to the Silhouette Desire hero—our **MAN OF THE MONTH!**

Sexy, macho, charming, irritating . . . irresistible! Nothing can stop these men from sweeping you away. Created by some of your favorite authors, each man is custom-made for pleasure—*reading* pleasure—so don't miss a single one.

Mr. January is Blake Donavan in RELUCTANT FATHER by Diana Palmer
Mr. February is Hank Branson in THE GENTLEMAN INSISTS by Joan Hohl
Mr. March is Carson Tanner in NIGHT OF THE HUNTER by Jennifer Greene
Mr. April is Slater McCall in A DANGEROUS KIND OF MAN by Naomi Horton
Mr. May is Luke Harmon in VENGEANCE IS MINE by Lucy Gordon
Mr. June is Quinn McNamara in IRRESISTIBLE by Annette Broadrick

And that's only the half of it—
so get out there and find your man!

Silhouette Desire's

MAN OF THE MONTH . . .

COMING IN APRIL

NAVY BLUES
Debbie Macomber

Between the devil and the deep blue sea . . .

At Christmastime, Lieutenant Commander Steve Kyle finds his heart anchored by the past, so he vows to give his ex-wife wide berth. But Carol Kyle is quaffing milk and knitting tiny pastel blankets with a vengeance. She's determined to have a baby, and only one man will do as father-to-be—the only man she's ever loved . . . her own bullheaded ex-husband! Can the wall of bitterness protecting Steve's battered heart possibly withstand the hurricane force of his Navy wife's will?

You met Steve and Carol in NAVY WIFE (Special Edition #494)— you'll cheer for them in NAVY BLUES (Special Edition #518). (And as a bonus for NAVY WIFE fans, newlyweds Rush and Lindy Callaghan reveal a surprise of their own. . . .)

Each book stands alone—together they're Debbie Macomber's most delightful duo to date! Don't miss

NAVY BLUES
Available in April,
only in *Silhouette Special Edition.*
Having the "blues" was never
so much fun!

SE518-1